A HEART MENDED

JESSIE SALISBURY

SOUL MATE PUBLISHING

New York

A HEART MENDED

Copyright©2014

JESSIE SALISBURY

Cover Design by Leah Suttle

This book is a work of fiction. The names, characters, places, and incidents are the products of the author's imagination or are used fictitiously. Any resemblance to actual events, business establishments, locales, or persons, living or dead, is entirely coincidental.

All rights reserved. No part of this publication may be reproduced, stored in a retrieval system, or transmitted in any form or by any means (electronic, mechanical, photocopying, recording, or otherwise) without the prior written permission of both the copyright owner and the publisher. The only exception is brief quotations in printed reviews.

The scanning, uploading, and distribution of this book via the Internet or via any other means without the permission of the publisher is illegal and punishable by law. Please purchase only authorized electronic editions, and do not participate in or encourage electronic piracy of copyrighted materials.

Your support of the author's rights is appreciated.

Published in the United States of America by
Soul Mate Publishing
P.O. Box 24
Macedon, New York, 14502

ISBN: 978-1-61935-935-2

ebook ISBN: 978-1-61935-631-3

www.SoulMatePublishing.com

The publisher does not have any control over and does not assume any responsibility for author or third-party websites or their content.

For all of my grandchildren:

Christy, Amy, Cassie, Bonnie, Justin, Robert, and Sarah

Acknowledgements

No book is written without help and I want to thank my first readers, Heather Pries and Stephanie Roper, who found the errors and inconsistencies, and my writing group, The Talespinners, for all of their prodding and encouragement.

1. WILFRED

Wilfred Bonneville had work to do, work that he had put off for too long, for most of the past winter, and it was now too late to do it. He put his hand on the head of the Irish setter sprawled beside him, sighed, and leaned his shoulder against the side of the old barn behind him. Below him, the sun rising behind the tall trees beyond the hill across the lake was turning the shadowed silver mist on Pleasant Pond into gold, his favorite time of day. Not wanting to move, he considered the building beside him. It had once been the barn used by the farm that was now Camp Rocky Point, the only original building left. The farm house below him and out of his sight had been so extensively remodeled into the camp offices, first-aid station, meeting room, and storage rooms, Wilfred could not think of it as a farmhouse. The big plank-sided barn, however, was much as it had always been.

Still reluctant to leave the view and the quietness, he pulled open the barn's plank door, moving slowly and carefully to avoid making any exertion that would bring pain. He did not want to resort to medication this early in the morning. The interior of the building was cobwebby and dusty, and one side still showed part of the stanchions that had once held a line of cows. The floor was piled haphazardly with leftovers from repair jobs done during the spring: shingles, broken furniture, a pile of cot mattresses that had been replaced with new ones but had not yet been disposed of. Wooden apple boxes that should have been returned to the orchard from which had come were piled untidily against the back wall. It still smelled of old barn boards and musty hay with a lingering scent of long-gone animals. The ground floor of the barn should have been cleared before the campers arrived, but Wilfred had not gotten around to it, put it off too long and now it was too late.

He didn't step over the crumbling board that formed the high threshold. To do the job now, to move all of those things to the upper level, would leave him in no condition to register campers, or to do anything else the camp director decided was his job. And his job was, according to his contract, watchman, counselor, and nature adviser. That he did many other things, as all the staff did, was beside the point. And clearing out this barn was a job that had been given him quite a while ago.

"I know the barn is off limits to campers," the camp director, Miss Amanda Lucey, had said, "but you never know about kids."

No, Wilfred thought, you never know about kids, what they are apt to do. *Especially the kids that end up at a camp like Rocky Point.*

He felt rather than heard someone beside him, heard the dog's tail thumping on the ground and then a gentle hand touched his arm. A soft voice said, "Will?"

He turned toward her. Petite, dark-haired camp nurse Shannon Conley, the only person he allowed to call him Will. Her dark eyes were full of concern but she smiled at him.

"Will you come to breakfast now?"

He turned back toward the dimness of the barn and the job waiting there for him.

"Not now, Will," she said. "You can't do it now, any more than you could do it before."

He glanced sideways at her again. She alone, of all the staff, knew about his pain, the heart attack he had had three years ago. He could not hide it from an attentive nurse. "All right, Shannon."

He pulled the door shut again, locked it firmly with the nailed on wooden turn-button, and turned to follow her, but paused to look once more over the lake. The sun had risen enough so that the soft gold tint was gone from the air, the silver mist had dissipated, and the early summer day had begun in earnest. He released a long breath and followed her. The red dog ran on ahead of them.

"It isn't all that bad, Will, really," she said. "If it was, you wouldn't have put up with them for three years."

It was that bad, but he didn't say so. He knew there were few, if any, other places available to him. "I know."

She led him around the barn and along an uphill path that skirted the edge of the woods beyond, out of sight of the lake and the boys' cabins. They rounded a clump of young maples, and the lake came into view again, and another row of slab-sided cabins and a long low building with a wide porch, the dining hall. This was the girls' section of the camp, and Shannon occupied a cabin, a little larger than the campers', on the hillside above the dining hall.

She held the door open for Wilfred and followed him into her tiny and scrupulously neat kitchen, saying to the dog behind her, "Not you, Mick." The table was set for two, and the coffee maker was making the strangling noises indicating that it was ready. He breathed in the welcome aroma of fresh coffee.

He asked, "How did you know where to find me?"

She smiled, poured his coffee, took two glasses of orange juice from the tiny refrigerator, and put two slices of bread into the toaster. "You weren't in your cabin."

He sat down in his usual place but didn't say anything. She spoke little, and her silence was one of the many things about her that endeared her to him.

"First thing in the morning, you go walking. Since you didn't come for me, I knew you were off brooding someplace."

"How long did you look?"

"Not long. I know where you like to go."

He knew that and stirred sugar into his coffee, keeping his attention on his cup, trying not to see her. She was so terribly young and innocent. And he was so old and tired. The aroma of the toasting bread reminded him how hungry he was, that he had not fixed himself a cup of coffee before he went out. He frequently didn't.

She put his perfectly prepared, just the way he liked them, poached eggs on the buttered toast and set the plate in front of him. "You have to eat. It will be a long day."

"Too long."

"Do you feel all right now?"

He heard the note of anxiety in her voice, and it irritated him more than usual. She didn't have to take care of him. "I'm fine."

She faced him, frowning, studying him until he looked at her. "I don't think I believe you. You've been over exerting. Again."

"You aren't my keeper." He knew he was being cruel, hurting her, rejecting her kindness in self-defense.

"Someone has to be. You have been alone so long you've forgotten that someone can care."

"I manage."

"I know." She put her own plate on the table and sat opposite him. "We still have an hour or so. Miss Lucey will be hollering for us early today. She always does on opening day."

"She probably didn't even sleep last night." He thought of his own dream-tormented night and wished he had given in to the temptation of watching the moon rise with her, sitting on the hill above the lake until he was sleepy, but he hadn't dared give in.

"She slept," Shannon said. "I gave her a sleeping pill."

Wilfred wondered why. "Oh?" He didn't think Shannon would really go that far to insure a quiet night.

"She asked if I had any. She was rather tense. As usual"

Wilfred returned his attention to the breakfast he didn't really want, and ate mechanically, as much to satisfy Shannon as himself, but knowing he needed the food.

She reached across the table and put her hand on his wrist. "I worry about you and I hate to see you suffer."

He didn't answer and didn't look at her, but he was very conscious of the warm softness of her hand touching his.

"Have you had your check-up this month?"

He didn't answer. She knew that he hadn't gone to the clinic.

"Will," she said, "you have to. You know that."

He said, as gruffly as he could manage, "Shan, let me be."

"I am always letting you be." She studied him, her always expressive eyes dark and serious. "And I know what you are going to tell me. I am twenty-seven, and you are forty-two. And I tell you, Wilfred Bonneville, I don't care."

"You have to care, Shan. You know how I am."

"I know you need me. And I love you."

"You don't know me." He was tired, too tired to go through it all again with her. Because he loved her, too, and couldn't tell her.

"I have known you for two years. That is enough."

"What about the other forty years?"

"I don't care about them."

He knew there were tears in her eyes, although she was looking at her plate and he could see only the top of her head. A stray sunbeam made red highlights in her dark hair. The redness fascinated him, but he resisted the urge to put his hand in the thick hair tumbling over her face. He could feel a tightness beginning in his chest, and he released a long shuddering breath, gaining control of himself, and the spasm passed without the frequent excruciating pain.

She looked up at once, alarmed, and saw that he was all right. "Will, I'm sorry. I've upset you."

He picked up her hand and held it. "That is why,"

he said. "Why you have to care about those other years. There is no cure for me."

"I care about you," she said, and didn't add as she had once before, there may be new surgeries, new techniques, that would help. He had already rejected those. It was too late for him.

He released her hand, finished the last of his eggs, and drained his coffee cup. "I am going to take one last walk around," he said, pushing himself to his feet. "Before they come."

She picked up the dishes and put them in her sink, working quickly. "Let me come, too, please."

He wanted her company, and would not deny himself. "All right."

She walked beside him, slowing her pace to his easy stroll. They followed a meandering path among the girls' cabins, and down to their dock. He stood a few minutes on the board walk gazing out over the smooth water of the lake, and then turned to the graveled path along the shore toward the boys' unit where he worked and had his office. He stopped again on their dock and glanced in the direction of the boathouse a little farther down the beach, then toward the barn, up the hill along the row of rustic cabins.

"Why do you dislike the campers so much?" Shannon asked.

"I don't dislike them."

"Resent them, then."

"I don't resent them, either."

"What then? You don't enjoy this job."

"I don't like what parents do to their children."

"This is a good camp, well run. They have good experiences here."

He turned toward the water again, enjoying the view that usually calmed him. "There are only two kinds of kids who come here: those whose parents send them here because they think the camp will make them into something different, more athletic or something, or those pathetic little ones whose parents want to take a fancy vacation without them. They probably go to boarding school, too."

"Now, really. Some of the kids like it here."

He shrugged.

Somewhere, far off, a bell rang, jangling in the still air.

"Darn," Shannon said.

Will turned away from the view and toward the dining hall, the direction from which the distracting sound had come. "Miss Lucey calls," he said, trying not to show his reluctance to answer the summons.

"Um. First staff meeting of a new camp season."

"But will this one be any different, any better?"

She didn't comment.

They met in the big dining room and gathered around the wide fieldstone fireplace, a purely symbolic gesture as there was no fire and wouldn't be unless there was a prolonged period of rain. Amanda Lucey enjoyed symbolism. She was a tall, angular thirtyish woman, wide framed, and long armed. Her red-brown hair was pulled severely back into a bun at the nape of her neck, and she wore large dark-framed glasses, but she was not unattractive. She had a pleasant appearance, not quite jolly, and inspired confidence in the young campers. She was terribly efficient.

Will sat as far away from her as was possible for him to get, in one of the few chairs that had been provided. Shannon sat cross legged on the floor beside him. He didn't listen to Miss Lucey's opening speech: he had heard it before at too many other camp session openings. He instead turned his attention to this year's group of counselors, some of whom he had not yet met, the eager college kids, boys and girls, enthusiastic, optimistic, so full of life and energy. He was enveloped by a deep sadness. *I'm really too old for this.*

So he shifted his gaze to Shannon, and watched her listening to Miss Lucey, seeing her thoughts register on her sensitive face: amusement at Miss Lucey's grandiloquent phrases, agreement with cautions, exasperation with the repetitions, and finally boredom as Miss Lucey continued. He glanced at the clock over the fireplace. It was almost time for the camp to open. He listened to Miss Lucey again, wondering where he would be put.

"Dan, you're in charge of seeing that all the boys find their cabins. Nancy, you do the same for the girls. Joyce and Susan will be checking in. Perry, you'll help Miss Conley with the boys check-ups. Fred . . ."

Will met her gaze, not smiling, to show his disapproval of the name she used.

Miss Lucey wavered a moment, then changed her tone to one less imperative. "Mr. Bonneville, would you be willing to stay here and talk to parents? You're a bit older, and—"

Will laughed. "Sure, why not?" It was the last thing he wanted to do. He couldn't stand campers' parents.

Shannon spoke up. "Miss Lucey, wouldn't it be better if he was down in the craft house? I mean, that's where he works, and somebody should be there."

That is a good idea," Miss Lucey said after a long moment. "I should have thought of it." She was again all brisk business. "Everybody up now and at 'em!"

Will got up and offered his hand to Shannon. "Up and at 'em, Miss Conley. The thundering horde is approaching."

She grimaced and followed him outside without commenting.

He glanced sideways at her. "Thanks."

There was the hint of a smile in her eyes, but her face stayed serious. "Do be careful, Will, please. Don't overdo."

"I never do."

She didn't answer, but he could see that she didn't agree. He patted her shoulder and turned away. "Get into that pretty uniform of yours so you can be the proper professional that you are."

"Pretty? Me? In scrubs?"

"Pretty to me."

"At least she lets me wear colors."

"Blue. It becomes you. Or one of those flowered ones. They look like you, cheerful."

"Will . . ."

"Have to take Mick home," he said, ignoring her concern. "I'll see you this evening."

The craft house was a plain and sturdy slab-sided structure, meant for rainy-weather activities. Across the front was a wide porch with a low railing made for sitting on, and inside were exposed beams, a field stone fire place at one end, and a low platform stage at the other. Benches ranged along the walls with a few chairs and small tables. A tiny room behind the stage served as Wilfred's office, where he kept his field books, charts, and whatever specimens his unit was studying, be it pond water denizens or fern fronds. He found a guide book to mosses and other non-flowering plants to read and sat down on the porch to await the arrival of the new bunch of little terrors.

He reviewed the first day's schedule: registration in the morning, cabin assignments, introductions and lunch, followed by afternoon swimming tests, orientation, supper, and a big evening campfire program put on by the counselors, except for him. He rarely took part in such events. He had only to speak about his own program: nature walks and study. He sat back and tried to enjoy the book, but he couldn't focus on it.

He wondered, as he often did, how long he would be tolerated in this position. There were younger men, much more enthusiastic than he, who would like the job, men who would take a much more active part in the camp life. He knew his only real asset was his willingness to live at the camp all year round, something a younger man might not want to do, that a college student couldn't do, and most of the counselors were college students.

He heard the new campers long before he saw any of them. They were loud, louder than he remembered from previous years, and he could see boys running around among the cabins and back and forth to the docks. Eventually several boys wandered to the craft house and asked what it was. They were about twelve years old, the average age of Rocky Point first session campers, all dressed in new dark green camp shorts and white tee shirts, Rocky Point Camp emblazoned across the front in glaring green. Will wondered how long those gleaming shirts, or the boys who were wearing them, would look so pristine.

He had long ago declined to wear the shorts and white shirts decreed for counselors. He had insisted, fairly politely, that a dark green, long-sleeved uniform such as he had worn as a forest ranger was much more appropriate for his job, for walking in the woods. He had not mentioned his age. Miss Lucey had reluctantly agreed.

"This is the craft house," Will told them. "Its name is Kaflick, a Native American word said to mean great works of nature. I'm Mr. Bonneville, your nature teacher."

"What do you do?"

"We go for walks in the woods and along the water, learn the names of the plants and trees. See what there is out there to look at."

"Bird walks, too? We did that at the last camp I went to."

"Sometimes."

"Yuck."

Will took that comment as a sign of a not very interested camper. "There are a lot of interesting facts to learn out there."

"Can we go inside?"

"Go ahead."

Later that evening Will sat in the gathering darkness at one side of the campfire, well away from the collected campers, and watched the opening ceremonies from the shadows. He had been introduced, made his usual speech about the beauties of the forest and field, and retired to the sidelines. It amused him, in a wry sort of way, that he would be Mr. Bonneville, whereas the others were Mr. Dan and Miss Joyce. He felt his age.

Eventually Shannon sat beside him.

"And how is the nursing business?" he asked.

"Fine, so far. I have my fingers crossed. This looks like a good group and none of them have special problems or medications I have to deal with."

"Day one went much better than usual, I thought." *I had no pain,* he meant.

"I see you have an early hike tomorrow. I wish Miss Lucey wouldn't give you hikes."

"Walking is good for me." She didn't comment, so he added, "I can pick my own routes and my own speed. We walk slowly so we can talk about everything we find. I don't climb mountains. That's Dan's pastime."

Someone near the fire had gotten up to speak and Will's attention was drawn away from Shannon toward the children sitting around the fire circle. He noticed a boy who sat alone at the edge of the firelight, withdrawn from the others, a slim, almost skinny boy with blondish hair and thin features. The flickering light gave him an almost feminine softness and put his profile in sharp relief. The expression on his face was one of sadness as if he were ready to cry. Will felt a sudden kinship with him, with his aloneness, and wondered why.

Miss Lucey began teaching the camp's goodnight song, the one that would be sung at each evening's fire circles. He returned his attention to Shannon sitting beside him. "Shall we get together later? Talk about all this?"

She smiled at him, silently agreeing that she would do whatever he asked.

"I have to walk back through the unit with the boys."

The campfire circle began to break as campers stood up and looked around. The girls gathered together in groups of three or four and moved away noisily with their unit leaders. The boys formed into a more straggling line. The sad-faced boy waited until the others had all started walking away before he rose to follow a short distance behind them.

Will stepped into the line beside him. "Hi, who are you?"

The boy stared up at him, startled. "Robert Sullivan."

"Robert?" Will smiled. "Do they call you Bobby?"

The boy shook his head. "Robbie."

"Is something wrong? are you sick?"

"No. I'm all right." He spoke fiercely, holding himself very straight.

"Homesick, already?"

"No."

Will put his hand on the boy's shoulder, a gesture he usually did not make. "Everyone gets that way, Rob. Don't worry about it."

In the harshness of the moonlight Wilfred thought the boy's face looked familiar, reminding him of someone. He shrugged off the feeling. "Believe me," he said, "this isn't a bad place."

"But I didn't want to come. I hate camp."

Will heard the misery in the boy's voice and sympathized. "I guess that can't be helped. I don't like it much myself, sometimes."

Robbie sputtered, "But, you work here."

"I live here." The boy's somehow familiar face continued to bother him even when seen in a different light, and the similarity was stirring up feelings Will thought he had forgotten many years ago. "What do have you against camp?"

"Nothing. My folks are going to Bermuda."

"Oh."

The boy stopped by a cabin. "I live here. Are you Mr. Bonneville, the nature teacher?"

"Yup."

"Sometimes I like that part. Can you teach me the names of the butterflies?"

"Yes, but why?"

He shrugged. "They're interesting and I'd just like to know their names."

"If you want," Will said, and wondered again why, why was he standing here talking to this boy with the disturbing face? "Good night, Robbie."

"Good night, Mr. Bonneville."

Will slowed his steps to a leisurely stroll as he walked up the hill to where his own cabin stood half hidden by a clump of birches. There was no need to hurry and he wanted to conserve his energy, but before he got to his cabin he was gripped by the terrifying constriction in his chest, the nearly unbearable agony of angina. He found his bottle of pills in his shirt pocket, shook one out and put it under his tongue, but it was a long minute before the seizure eased, leaving him shaken and gasping for breath. He leaned against a tree and breathed deeply until he could stand normally again. Then he whistled for his dog, went to a place he knew, picked a handful of field daisies, and returned, angling across the top of the hill to where Shannon was waiting for him.

2. ROBBIE

Going into his assigned cabin was about the last thing Robbie Sullivan wanted to do. He stood at the bottom of the steps debating what he should do and knowing that he had no options. There was no place else to go and no one he could complain to, since he hadn't yet spent a night with them. He had taken a good look at his five cabin-mates before supper and knew he wouldn't like them, nor would they like him. He had been to enough camps to know that. He simply wasn't like them and they would quickly realize that and act on it.

But he couldn't stay outside forever. He trudged up the four plank steps and pushed open the door. He had arrived first and had chosen the bottom bunk nearest the door. His duffle bag was still there with his pillow, and his foot locker was underneath, just as he had left them. That was encouraging, because sometimes his cabinmates had moved his belongings, hidden them, or tied his clothes in knots. This year he still had that to look forward to, as much as he hoped it wouldn't happen.

He slipped into his bunk and lay still, watching the others in the room. They were playing cards, completely engrossed, and didn't see him. He remembered their names, but not which name went with which face: Sam, Joe, Bert, Art, and Corey. He hoped at least one of them would be friendly. There had been little opportunity in his life to learn how or experience making friends quickly. He had no brothers or sisters, no close cousins. He had moved several times in his twelve years, and had few friends at home. He was not athletic and didn't want to be. He couldn't swim, detested soccer and wasn't interested in playing baseball or football. Given a choice, he preferred to sit and watch.

He would rather have gone to Bermuda with his parents. Last year they'd gone to California, and the year before that to Hawaii. All three times, Robbie had gone to camp. Twice he had gone to the same camp. This year he had protested, and here he was at Rocky Point.

"You need to get to know some other kids," his mother had said. "Get out in the fresh air."

"You sit around and read too much," his father said. "You should play baseball, exercise more. You're too thin and pale."

Robbie had tried to protest, but his parents had not listened. Camp would be good for him, they'd said.

"This time," his father said, "play games. Get out there and do things with other kids. And learn to swim."

"You'll have a good time," his mother had said this morning, before he had left with his father to come here. "Rocky Point is highly recommended. It's a good camp. There'll be nice boys for you to play with."

Lying quietly on his bunk, Robbie considered his cabin-mates again, trying to determine what they might be like. They were all bigger than he was, taller or heavier, or both, but he did not think that they were older. They were playing a very noisy game of cards.

The game came to a crashing end, cards scattered around, with much laughter, and during the general picking-up which followed, one of the boys noticed Robbie.

"Hey, our cabin-mate is back. Where you been?"

"Outside." Robbie tried not to sound evasive. "Looking around."

"I didn't see you at the campfire."

The voice was accusing and Robbie was instantly defensive. "I was there." He pointed at the biggest one he thought was named Bert. "You were part of the Indian dance."

They agreed that he had been at the campfire. "Do you want to play cards with us?"

He didn't, but he asked, "What are you playing?"

"I Doubt It. Do you know it?"

Robbie did, so he got off the bunk and joined the circle. He sat a little apart from the other boys, not touching anyone, as the cards were dealt. The play started to his right, and when it reached him, he had a three, named it and put it down quickly. The play continued around the circle with much hooting but without actual challenge, until it returned to him. He did not have the required nine and hesitated, then put a queen down quickly saying, "One nine."

But he had hesitated too long, and Bert challenged immediately, crowing. "I doubt it!"

Robbie scooped up the cards in the center of the table without turning over his queen, and began to sort them into his hand. He felt his face burning. He didn't listen to the others and so didn't know what card was wanted when his turn came again.

"Twos," Sam said.

Robbie hurriedly fished out three cards and put them down. He was immediately challenged. He turned over two twos and three. He opened his mouth to speak, but nothing came out.

With all the cards again heaped haphazardly in front of him, he had no choice but to pick them all up. He knew he could now challenge almost any play, but he didn't, not even Corey when he slapped down his last card calling it a seven. It was easier not to, easier to not say or do anything.

In the ensuing noisy confusion , their redheaded counselor, who Robbie recalled was Mr. Perry, stuck his head in the door. "Okay, guys, fifteen minutes. Get up to the wash house."

Thankfully, Robbie got up, found his soap and towel, toothbrush, and pajamas, and fled into the covering darkness.

He managed to be the last to return to the cabin, coming in just as Mr. Perry, was checking the bunks.

"You almost didn't make it, kid," Perry said.

Robbie crawled into his bunk and covered his head with the pillow.

Soon after breakfast, in the coolness of a beautiful morning, Robbie walked a few paces behind Mr. Bonneville along a twisting path through the woods above the camp. He had a small notebook with him and made such notes in it as he thought necessary, although he noticed that most of the other boys were apparently not listening, few had notebooks, and none were taking notes. They had been walking leisurely for the better part of an hour, and Mr. Bonneville had been naming the trees for them, pointing out distinguishing marks. They had examined leaves and bark on several kinds of trees, counted growth rings in the stump of a recently cut tree, and looked at the various lichens that grew on the trees and rocks. He had shown them birds' nests, holes made by woodpeckers in a dead stub, and a poplar stump that had been chewed by beavers.

The outing left Robbie enthralled and wanting more. Other nature guides had shown him many of these same things, but they had lacked Mr. Bonneville's quiet enthusiasm and his apparently vast store of knowledge of fascinating details. They stood finally at the edge of the woods on a hillside overlooking the camp. "There we are, boys, home again, and it's warm enough to go swimming." Mr. Bonneville gestured toward the lake. "And your instructor seems to be waiting on the dock."

With a whoop, the boys started down the hill, yelling and racing each other. Robbie lingered and glanced around seeking for an excuse to ask a question, make a comment, anything that would delay the hated swimming a few minutes. Beside the path was the crumbling remains of a large pine tree, cut in some distant past and now mostly rotted and covered with a thick, gray-green growth.

Robbie knelt for a closer look, intrigued that some of the tiny gray stems were tipped with bright red, a type of moss he had never noticed before. He picked up a piece of the crumbling wood for closer inspection. "Mr. Bonneville, what's this stuff?"

The counselor turned and looked at the piece of wood in Robbie's hand. "British soldiers."

Robbie gaped at him in disbelief.

"British soldiers, red coats, because of the red caps on them and the way the stalks stand up like little soldiers. Actually, it's called red crested lichen, one of the fruticose lichens found on decayed wood. It's very common around here."

Mr. Bonneville's voice was friendly and Robbie was encouraged. "I like red coats."

"So do I. But I think it's time for your swimming class."

Robbie got up, brushed dirt off his knees. "You said you'd tell me the names of the butterflies."

"I will, when we see some."

Robbie had to be satisfied with that. He handed the piece of lichen covered wood to the counselor and slowly walked down to the docks where once again he would be classed as a non-swimmer, a beginner with the youngest campers. At the close of a long day which ended with a noisy evening hike along the edge of the lake with Mr. Dan and Mr. Perry he returned to his cabin hoping it was time for lights out.

He found the cabin empty, the others apparently having gone to the wash house already. He also found his pajamas tied to the bunk post with his pajama strings, wound tightly with many knots. He made no attempt to untie them and slept in his shorts.

3. WILFRED

Will closed his office door and walked through Kaflik to the porch, carrying the piece of crumbling wood with the cluster of red coats Robbie had picked up. He thought of the boy who had given it to him, who had asked such uncharacteristic questions. A non-athletic type, he thought, sent to camp by his parents to be made into the outdoors type. It would never work. And he had such a sad face. Little boys should not have sad faces. And Robbie's face was still vaguely familiar, still reminding him of someone he didn't remember. He pushed the thought aside. If it was important, it would come to him later, and he could see no reason why it should be.

He'd had a long and trying day, and there was peace and rest in the little cabin at the other side of the camp if he wanted it. There was almost anything there that he might want. He had only to ask, but he couldn't ask. She offered so much that he could not take. Accepting that offering would not be fair to Shannon. He turned toward her cabin anyway, trudging up the hill past the boys' cabins. He heard their voices, laughter, and singing, but no distinct words.

Their muted voices blended not unpleasantly with the sounds and smells of the pleasantly cool evening: the deep-throated wanging of the bull frogs, a hunting owl away off on the high hill somewhere, the sleepy twittering of a bird returned to its nest. The breeze flowing from the lake was cool, dispelling the mosquitoes and bringing with it the scent of new mown hay from a distant farm. Fireflies flitted and twinkled in the grasses around him and he was not too dissatisfied with his world. At the top of the hill he stopped, whistled, and waited until Mick the Irish setter joined him, tail wagging and eager for an evening ramble..

There was a welcoming light in Shannon's cabin, but she was not there. He put the piece of lichen covered wood on her kitchen table, in front of a mayonnaise jar full of field daisies. He smiled at the cheerful bouquet that was so like her. He stepped outside and sat on her steps with the old dog sprawled at his feet. There was a light in the dining hall, and he supposed Miss Lucey was holding a conference, a recap of the day's activities, or there was one of the occasional counselor get-togethers. Relaxing in the quietness brought on one of his occasional longings for the cigarette he could no longer have.

He rested his chin on his hand, absorbing the hundred varying chirps and twitterings of the evening, but he could not sit still. The insistent desire for the cigarette drove him to his feet again, and he sauntered across the brow of the hill toward his own cabin. He did not want to stay there, either, so he headed for the boys' dock. Sitting by the water was usually calming.

Before they reached the line of cabins, Mick found a boy sitting huddled under a tree. "What are you doing out here?" Will asked, more gruffly than he intended. There shouldn't be any campers out here alone in the dark.

"They locked me out." Robbie's gaze was on the dog.

"Who? How?"

"My cabinmates when I went to the john."

"Where's your counselor?"

"I don't know. They said if I told him they'd beat me up."

Will let out a long breath, and calmed himself. "Come on, Robbie. We'll go find Mr. Perry."

There was a light in the counselor's cabin. Will rapped once, and pulled the door open. Perry and Joyce were both in the bunk, arms around each other.

Perry turned around, his anger obvious.

"Sorry, Joyce," Will said. "Perry has a problem. Robbie's been locked out by his mates."

Perry got up, grumbling and came outside. "Why didn't you just make them let him back in?"

"This is your unit. And Robbie has to survive with them. You have to discover this sort of thing, without their knowing that he told you."

"Well, since he's here, and I have to get him back in, how do you propose I keep it a secret?" He did not attempt to veil his sarcasm.

"Oh, for Pete's sake," Will said. "Just go make a cabin check. If Robbie comes in while you are there, he can simply say he went to the john alone because he couldn't wake anybody up."

"If the door is locked, how do you explain that?"

"They will have an explanation. Accept it. Kids always have an explanation."

Perry grumbled something unintelligible, and followed Will into the shadows between the cabins. Robbie trailed along, saying nothing, the dog walking beside him wagging his long tail.

Perry walked up the cabin steps and pushed on the door. When it refused to open, he rattled it. "Come on, you guys, unblock the door."

There were sounds of muffled voices, of something heavy being dragged, and then the door opened a few inches and someone looked out.

Perry pushed his way in and turned on the light. He stood in the doorway, obviously counting. "Where's the other one . . . Rob?"

"I don't know. We thought everyone was here."

"What's the idea of the foot lockers in front of the door?"

"The guys in the next cabin said they was going to raid us."

Will gave Robbie a small push toward the cabin. "Go on," he whispered. "And look innocent."

Robbie walked into the light and said, "Hi. What's going on?"

"Bed check," Perry said. "Where in hell were you?"

"John."

"You're not supposed to go alone."

"I was in a hurry, and nobody would wake up."

The excuses sounded strange so early in the evening, but Will left Perry to accept the explanations as the easiest way out of the situation. No longer wanting to sit on the dock since the desire for a cigarette had faded, Will turned away from the cabin and climbed back up the hill. "Come on, Mick, let's get out of here. It's Perry's problem, not ours."

He sat down by the corner of the old barn and relaxed against it. The lowest rim of the sky glowed palely green in the faint light lingering in the western sky from the vanished sunset and no sounds from the camp reached him. He let his mind float free while he absorbed the coolness and the peace of the night. The freshening breeze stirring the trees near him brought with it the scent of field flowers and damp grass. The low moon reflected softly in the lake below him, its image distorted by the ripples raised by the breeze, breaking the moon into several wavering stripes. The fireflies danced along the path, and he could hear the distant croak of a bullfrog. He again wanted the cigarette. He hadn't had one in years, not since his nearly fatal heart attack. He didn't want to move, so Will thought of Shannon instead: so young, so eager, so loving, so unattainable. How could he give her what she wanted? Even if he had his health, Shannon was not for him. Not now, not ever. It was too late for that, for him ever to love anyone again.

How long had it been, he wondered, since he had given his love to someone? Ten years? Twelve? Twelve years at least since Carol . . . years he had been alone, his soul too shattered to trust anyone enough to love again. Even to

Shannon, who would be so easy to love, who offered her love so openly, he could not give in return.

Three years earlier, before his heart attack, he had been attracted to a young woman named Barbara, a pretty, outgoing co-worker, and he had taken her out a few times. He had begun to think he could come to love her as he had Carol, but Barbara had not survived his illness. He had not returned to his work, had taken a leave of absence from the Forest Service, and he had not heard from her since. Her desertion was another brick in the wall he had built around himself, a wall that he could safely hide behind.

But as he had not in many years, he thought of Carol, the girl who had been his wife, the high-spirited golden girl who loved to dance and party, and who had no use at all for the quietness of the forest; the girl who had a face like Robbie's . . .

A sudden tightening and an agonizing searing pain tore at his chest, bringing with it a terrifying shortness of breath. He rolled over onto the grass, grasping in his pocket for his life-saving pills.

The dog pushed at him with his nose and whined.

4. SHANNON

Shannon left the dining hall as soon as she could gracefully escape and jogged up the path toward her cabin, relieved to be out of a stifling staff meeting and into the quiet and comforting darkness. She thought, *Miss Lucey can sure be a long-winded bore, seeing that she went over all of that yesterday.* But since Shannon really wanted to stay here at the camp to be near Will, there wasn't anything to do but quietly endure Miss Lucey's way of running it.

She hoped that Will would be waiting for her, sitting on her cabin steps, but she knew that he wouldn't be. He didn't like to sit quietly and wait, even for her. She was thankful he was not required to attend the meetings that Miss Lucey called so frequently. He had said, logically enough Shannon thought, someone had to be out and around to keep an eye on the campers, so he rarely attended and the other counselors took turns.

As she had known, Will was not sitting on her steps. She picked up the piece of lichen-covered wood he had left on her table, warmed by the thought he had been there and had been thinking of her wherever he had found the piece of old wood. She put it back where he had left it, in front of his gift of field daisies, and went into the starlit night again. She paused on the steps, wondering which of several places he might be, places he liked to sit. She decided on a route that would lead her to all of his favorite spots in an easy, logical course, starting with his cabin.

As she walked, she thought about Will, his thinness, the gray so prominent in his sun-streaked blondish hair, the almost delicate features of his face. Her love for him was warm, bubbling through her being. Her affection for him had grown slowly over the past two years as she had come to know him, in spite of his withholding himself from her and the world. She knew about his hidden side, the deep and unexplained sadness, his great store of knowledge of the natural world, but mostly she knew his gentle kindness.

But she also knew his pain, the residue of a heart attack for which he took medication, but about which he refused to talk.

Will was a quiet man, a warm, giving person trying to hide from something in his past that had hurt him terribly. She wondered what it was, but she could not ask. If she asked, he would simply withdraw further, and perhaps shut her out entirely. She knew only that a woman had hurt him, had caused him to suspect all women, made him keep his love to himself, not trusting anyone with his inner feelings. He hadn't told her anything, but the truth was there for her to see in small things he said, or large things left unsaid. Her heart ached for him. And for herself. She had come to know him one small piece at a time, through a casual comment in an unguarded moment. He gave so reluctantly of himself, she treasured each little piece.

She found his cabin empty, as she had known it would be. She did not go in but stood for a moment on the steps, absently petting Charlie, the big white cat lying as usual on the porch rail, as she wondered which of several other places he might be. She turned toward the lake, walking slowly, enjoying the cool stillness of the evening and quiet whirring of unseen insects, still thinking of Will, his silence about his past, and his apparent inability to talk about himself.

She knew that somewhere on the hillside, Will was watching the moon's shimmering, broken reflection in Pleasant Pond. The desire to be with him grew, and she hurried to a vantage point ahead of her. The boys' dock was empty, the post against which Will liked to lean solitary in the moonlight. Since Will had not chosen the dock, she looked back up the hill. Had he chosen lean against the side of the old barn, or the ledge above his cabin?

The barn was closer, so she went that way. She heard Mick's distress before she reached it, and started running, fear gripping her stomach, shortening her breath.

Will was face down in the grass.

She knelt beside him, the hard knot tightening in the pit of her chest. "Will?"

She put her hands on his shoulder, gently easing him onto his back. His eyes were closed and his face drawn, deathly pale in the moonlight. Her fingers on his wrist found his pulse, and it was steady. Relieved, she said, "Will?"

He opened his eyes and recognized her.

"Will, what happened?"

He put his hand on her arm, and almost smiled. "Just a seizure," he said, so softly she scarcely heard him. "I'll be all right in a minute."

"Oh, Will!" Her arms encircled his shoulders, and she held his head against her breast.

He attempted feebly to push himself away from her. "I'm all right now." His voice was a little stronger. "Let me be."

But she didn't want to let him go. She had so few chances to touch him, other than his hand. "Take it easy, Will. Rest a moment."

"Shannon, let me go."

The familiar hurting hardness was back in his voice.

She released him and watched him maneuver himself carefully into a sitting position and then lean against the wall of the barn with his eyes closed. "What happened, Will?"

"Nothing. Just an attack."

She knew that he wanted no expressed sympathy so she tried to use her professional voice, the one she used with the campers. "Something brings them on. What were you doing?"

"Just sitting here." He opened his eyes and managed a smile. "Sometimes they just happen. You know that."

In the paleness of the moonlight his face appeared as a sickly pallor. She wondered if it really were that color, how he really felt. "Will . . ."

A flicker of pain crossed his face, visible even in the dim light. "Shan, please, don't call me Will."

She wondered what he had against the name, who had once called him that and had hurt him so deeply. She knew that he allowed no one else to use it. She said, "All right, if that is what you want."

He closed his eyes again, but his breathing was almost normal. She knew then he had taken his pills and was relieved.

She put her hand in his, but without saying his name, she didn't know how to speak to him. He detested the shortening of his name to Fred and Wilfred seemed so cold and formal.

"I'm sorry," he said, his eyes still closed but his voice stronger. "She called me Will."

She squeezed his fingers, but still could say nothing. What had made him think of her, whoever she was? The one who hurt him so?

He sat with his head bent, breathing deeply and more easily, and she knew that his medication was taking effect.

"Wilfred?" she said gently.

"It doesn't sound right for you to say Wilfred. Only my mother called me that." He raised his head and looked at her. "It's not your fault."

"If you want to talk about it . . ."

He pushed himself straighter, moved his shoulders tentatively, and leaned against the barn again. "No."

She still held his hand, and looked at his strong tanned fingers encircling hers instead of at him. "Sometimes it helps."

"Her name was Carol," he said slowly, carefully, "I was married to her for a little over two years."

Shannon could think of no answer for that. *What made him think of her now?*

"Someone reminded me of her," he said, closing his eyes again. "I hadn't thought about her, tried not to think about her, for ten years or better."

"Will . . ." She stopped. "I'm sorry. I forgot.'

"It doesn't matter. You don't say it like she did, anyway." He opened his eyes, turned his head enough to look at her. "Shan, just sit there and look pretty. Don't ask me questions I can't answer."

"All right. If that is what you want."

"That's what I want." He closed his eyes again, but also tightened his fingers around her hand.

She sat silently, watching him closely, professionally, seeing his breathing grow more regular, less labored. She could not tell if the color were returning to his face. The moonlight made him look ghastly. She convulsively closed her hand around his.

He opened his eyes and met hers again. "I'm all right now, Shan. Don't worry."

"But I do, Will, all the time."

He straightened and reached for her other hand. "You mustn't," he said. "Not ever."

"But why? I love you."

"You can't. I messed up everything for her, and I won't do it to you."

"Everyone makes mistakes. You just have to pick up all the pieces and start over. Your life didn't end . . . when you and she parted, did it?"

He looked down at her hand still clasped in his and didn't answer.

"You are still alive, Will. You can't mope around forever. Whatever happened between you, it makes no difference to me. It never will. That is all over and past."

"You don't understand."

"I might, if you explained it to me."

He shook his head.

She got up and tugged at his arms. "Come. I think you'd better get back to your cabin, have something to drink and lie down."

He resisted. "Let me sit here awhile longer, Shan." He drew her down beside him into the circle of his arm.

She buried her face in his shoulder, surprised at his boniness, but comforted by the pressure of his arm around her waist. She could feel strength in his arm that was not obvious in looking at him. She wondered why his usual cold reserve had vanished, but did not question it. She was where she had often longed to be.

He put his hand on her shoulder, lightly caressed her arm for a moment, then moved his hand to her hair. "She had blond hair," he said softly, "long, golden hair that hung down her back in big waves. I don't think it was natural, but it was beautiful."

Sudden unbidden tears stung her eyes and to hide any emotion from him, she pressed her face tighter against his shoulder.

He went on, speaking with very little feeling.. "Her eyes were sort of greenish, I think. She always wore some kind of makeup to make them look greener." He paused, but Shannon didn't dare comment. "She was all like that, artificial. Nothing about her was honest. Your eyes are honest, Shan, big and brown, and deep, and everything you feel is right there for everyone to see. I never knew what she felt."

"Oh, Will."

"I loved her." His voice was dull, expressionless and she wondered how deep the hurt had gone, what it was that she, whoever she was, had done to him.

"And I love you, Will." Her voice was muffled by his shoulder.

He moved his arm away from her, abruptly releasing her from his embrace and put his hands on her shoulders, facing him. She sat a little straighter and met his intent gaze. Although his face was in shadow and she couldn't really see his eyes, she could feel his suppressed anger. He held her with both hands, away from him for a moment, not speaking, and then, suddenly, pulled her closer and kissed her, gently at first, and then harder.

He released her as suddenly as he'd grabbed her, and leaned back against the side of the barn, his eyes closed, and his face haggard in the soft white of the moonlight.

She tightened her fingers around his arm, still breathless from the impact of his kiss, his first, and the sudden release of all her stored emotions. "Will . . ."

"I'm sorry, Shannon. So sorry."

"Oh, don't be, Will, please. I've waited so long."

"It can't be," he said. "I can never love anyone again. Ever." He added after a long moment, "I have such a short time left to live."

"But it could be years, Will, if you take care of yourself."

"It could be tomorrow."

"I love you, Will. I want your remaining time to be happy, however long it is."

"I asked you not to speak of love to me, Shan. You promised."

"That was a long time ago." She picked up his unresisting hand and held it tightly in both of hers against her chest. "But, if that's what you want, I won't say it. You know it anyway."

"Yes," he said, "I know it, and she never did, not really. I was a means of escape for her, a way out of the life she had, a source of all the things she wanted."

Shannon wanted to ask what had happened to Carol, where she had gone, what she had done to Will, but she held her tongue and kept her eyes on the hand gripping hers so tightly he was hurting her fingers. And she wondered who had reminded him of his ex-wife, but she didn't dare ask.

Will didn't say anything more.

Shannon looked at him and her heart was torn by the agony on his face. "Are you in pain now?"

"No. The pain is gone, all of it. It always goes away."

He was breathing properly, so she knew that the pain now was of a different sort, a worse kind, which his medication could not ease, and she didn't know what to say to comfort him. "Shall we go back to your cabin now? I'll make you something to drink. You could use some coffee, or hot chocolate maybe."

"In a minute, Shan. Come here." He encircled her waist with his armagain, held her tight against his chest without really embracing her, just holding her as he might a sister. "You are a dear, Shan. You have done more for me than you'll ever know, but you are just a child. I'm an old man."

"I am not a child, and you are not old."

"I was married at twenty-nine," he said, ignoring her observation. "Before that I was too busy going to school, learning how to earn myself a living in the way I wanted to earn it. I had built myself a country house, the kind of comfortable, roomy place I wanted, had always dreamed about, out of logs and field stones on a hill under some big old oak trees, with a little brook running through the front yard, and beds of wildflowers."

"It sounds beautiful."

"It still is. I drove by it a few years ago, and it hasn't changed very much." He paused, remembering, "She lived there only long enough to find a buyer for it. Whoever bought it has taken good care of it."

She couldn't comment on that. There was too much hurt in his voice.

"I was divorced just before I was thirty-one. Twelve years ago. I haven't seen her since . . . since the day she made it plain she no longer wanted me." He added after a long pause, "If she ever did."

"And since then?"

"I worked with the Forest Service until I had the heart attack. We had no children, and she married someone else as soon as possible so I didn't have to support her. I had just me."

But you need someone, Will," she said very softly, "everybody needs someone."

"I don't really deserve anyone. What am I that someone could care for me? I failed her. I'm not going to fail anyone else."

"What did she do to you, to make you so bitter? You are a nice person, warm and generous, and kind, and you know so much about everything around us. Everyone likes you, Will, even Miss Lucey says it, how nice you are."

He hugged her, holding her tight in the circle of his arms, laughing gently at her, but the laugh was edged with a hard bitterness. "I was always a nice person, Shan. Everyone takes advantage of that kind of person. All of my life, it's been like that."

She rested her head against his chest, enjoying the warmth of his arms around her, wanting him to go on talking, but not daring to ask him, even though she knew that his talking would probably do him good.

"And look at you," he said, "so young and innocent. What do you know of the hard things in life?"

"Didn't you ever wonder why I started working here at this camp instead of some hospital someplace that would pay me a heck of a lot better?" She tried to keep the sadness out of her voice. "I came here running, looking for a place to hide. His name was Jimmie, and we'd been engaged for two years."

"Why such a long engagement and no wedding?"

"He didn't really want to get married. He just wanted a nice safe relationship, a Saturday night date. And then he met . . . another girl and married her. Just like that."

She let out a long shuddering breath, remembering the hurt, the shame of his abandonment. "I didn't think I'd ever trust another man, either." She raised her head and looked up at him. "Until I learned to know you. I know I can trust you completely."

"You can't know." His voice was flat, without hope.

"I know, Will. I know you."

"Didn't you know before . . . with Jimmie?"

"No, I only thought. When he left me I was shattered, devastated, but it was only my pride. I was actually relieved, after I stopped and thought about it."

"I loved Carol," he said, with so much sadness in his voice it tore her soul, "with all my heart."

She closed her eyes against the sudden tears and pressed her face tighter against his chest to relieve the sick hopelessness in the pit of her stomach. She asked, "Now? After all this time and whatever she did to you?"

"No, but now I can love no one."

Relief flooded her like a warm drink. She was not lost after all, there was still hope. "I have learned to love you," she said, "in spite of you and everything you've said, and I know you don't totally hate me."

"Hate you, Shan? You are the only good thing left in my life."

"Then let me love you and take care of you."

He kissed her check, and pushed her away from him. He got up slowly, carefully, and then offered her his hand. "I think it's time for me to go home."

The dog got up as well and padded beside them, his tail wagging.

Shannon kept her hand lightly in Will's, not saying anything because she knew that he liked her quietness so he could hear the night-sounds. She was so conscious of his nearness, of the light touch of his lips as they had brushed her check, she could hear none of the sounds around her that usually intrigued her.

He stopped her at the bottom of his cabin steps. "Good night Shan."

She looked at him, not comprehending what he had said.

"Good night," he said again. "And thanks. For everything."

His face was in dark shadow, and she could not see his eyes. "Will . . ."

"I don't think I can walk you home. Even for that cup of cocoa."

Concerned again about his seizure, she asked, "Are you all right? Has the pain come back?"

"I'm fine, Shan. Go home to bed like a good girl. Tomorrow will be another long day at good Camp Rocky Point."

She heard the hard note in his voice, knew his sometimes obvious dislike of his job. "Good night, Will. If you can't sleep, take something. You have a long day tomorrow, too."

He didn't answer her and she turned away, walked up the path, not looking back at him, his rejection hurting. She was almost home before she remembered: he held her in his arms and kissed her. He had not said he disliked her even if he had not said that he loved her.

She made herself a cup of peppermint tea, checked her schedule for the following day, noted she had a first aid class she needed to prepare for, although with such young campers it was not a very involved course. The class had been her suggestion last year and she enjoyed it, felt the campers gained at least a little knowledge from it.

It was late when she went to bed but sleep didn't come in spite of her tiredness. In a half-sleep state she recalled the past year, slowly realizing how much Will had come to mean to her, how much she would miss him if something happened.

And it could happen. At any time. Do I really want to stay with him and experience that? But, she told herself, *I don't really know the extent of his illness, what damage was done to his heart, what his prognosis is, just what he tells me, and that isn't very much, just what I've figured out. There could be new techniques if he would only try them.*

She forced herself to consider all of the possibilities. What would she do if they were together—she didn't go as far as thinking of marriage since Will had been so hurt by whatever that other marriage had done to him—if they were still here at the camp several years from now. *Not that I want to stay here at Rocky Pont forever. And neither does he.*

Shannon knew, deep down, that Will's early and sudden death was a possible, almost certain, future that she had to consider, think about, and decide if she really wanted to continue down that path, tie herself and her future to a man with a badly damaged heart.

But damaged in so many different ways. It isn't the physical harm that is holding him back.

She recalled again his arms around her, holding her against his chest, and she held onto that warm feeling, the sense of security she had felt there. She recalled his kiss, the stirring in her heart that it has caused, and she was sure. She would stay by Will no matter what came.

With that thought she considered the coming day and what it could bring, what she might make it bring. A new day had so many possibilities.

5. WILFRED

Will lay on his bunk with his eyes closed, trying not to remember either what had happened tonight or the memories of a more distant past it had stirred up. He willed himself to clear his mind and to fall sleep, but sleep was a long way off, and he knew it; he had lain awake through too many sleepless nights not to recognize the signs. He made a cup of hot chocolate he didn't want and took a hot shower, but he knew even those time-tested rituals wouldn't help. He tried to make himself relax, to think of those pleasant things he loved, the deep shadowy woods, quiet pathways lined with delicate ferns, murmuring brooks and clear sparkling lakes, but there had been too many recent events for him to consider.

So he thought of Shannon, visualizing her pert pixie face, but he could see nothing there but pain, the distress that he had caused her, as he had caused everybody pain. He considered her offered love, her soft yielding body pressed close to his, her warm and eager lips, and fervently wished he could take what she offered so freely. But he loved her too much to take it. *I will not hurt her like I've hurt everyone else.*

He loved Shannon, but not as he had loved Carol. His love then had been much younger, hot first love, an all-consuming passion. He had given himself completely to Carol, and her rejection of him had left him drained, a hollow shell with no feeling but shame and hatred. That had gradually dissipated but had left him empty and unable to love another. He knew, because he had tried it once and that, too, had failed.

No, he told himself firmly, he loved Shannon as he would a young sister, a soft, gentle, warm kind of love. He was too old, too sick, for burning ardor. A corner of his mind told him that he did not love her like a sister, could never love her that way, that she was a very desirable woman that he wanted, but he was too tired to acknowledge the thought.

He recalled Perry and Joyce as he had seen them in Perry's cabin. That was young love, uninvolved and abandoned, a thing of the moment to be enjoyed and forgotten. Last year Perry had had a girl named Wendy. Summer breaks were made for hot romance and it meant nothing to any to them.

Will was too old for such casual flings. Love had to mean something. *At least, it was supposed to mean something. Had his love ever meant anything to Carol? Why had she rejected everything he had offered her?*

He remembered what Shannon had said of her lost love, her broken engagement. She had been relieved when he was gone, in spite of the fact that she had run blindly to hide here from her loss and disappointment. Run away to here, Camp Rocky Point, to lick her wounds. He was grateful chance had brought her to the camp. Eternally grateful. Without Shannon, he would have given up long ago, yielded to the crushing pain and the overwhelming depression that had been choking him when she arrived. Without her, he would probably be in a hospital somewhere, or an institution, or dead. He had been headed that way.

He recalled their first meeting, two years ago. She had come to the camp a day early to get settled in, she said, to learn about the camp, how it operated, where she would be working. She had found him sitting by the old barn as he had been tonight, recovering from a seizure brought on by trying to do too much, as usual.

She had found his pills for him, had him lie down in the grass and relax. She sat beside him and talked quietly of many things while he calmed down. He wasn't as used to the searing pain then as he was now.

She had asked few questions, but he had sensed that he had told her a lot more than he intended to. She had that quiet quality that made her good with children, able to calm their fears. She had done the same for him. And was continuing to do it, quietly caring and watching out for him, in spite of his resistance.

He had seen little of Shannon during that first camp session, but she had come to him during the break between sessions, and sat on his steps with him, petting Charlie the cat and asking what he did. He had talked about trees and plant succession and pond life, all of the parts of his life work for the Forest Service, trying to discourage her.

He found her presence comforting, and he had warmed toward her, letting her thaw his resolve a little. He had admitted to himself that he was lonely. Mick and Charlie were merely comforting companions, not company.

"You work too hard," she'd said. "You need to set yourself a schedule that will get the jobs done without so much effort on your part. I will help, if you like." Her voice was mostly the professional nurse, but even then there had been more, a genuine concern for him.

But that concern had irritated him. "I'm sure I can manage."

She smiled up at him, her wide-eyed elfin grin. "Of course you can. You are a very competent person."

By the end of that summer she had become an important part of his life, but he had never said so, nor had she. During the winter while she lived elsewhere, working in a clinic in town, she had written to him faithfully. She had phoned a few times, and he liked the sound of her voice, but he found her letters comforting, something he could hold and reread. She had driven out to see him several times, to take him where he needed to go. Will had been denied a driver's license because of his heart, and he disliked asking for help. He had accepted her offers gratefully, but determined not to become dependent on her goodness.

Two summers with her, he thought. This one will be three. *I'm not being fair to her, but I can't let her go. She is the only good thing I know. She is much too good for me. What she needs is a healthy young man to take care of her, do the things she likes to do, not an old man with a bad heart liable to kick off any minute.*

Why, he asked himself as he had so many times, had he had a heart attack at thirty-nine? Heart attacks are supposed to happen to old people. But he knew the answer to that one: the rheumatic fever he'd had as a child left him with a weakened heart. Doctors had told him once or twice that a heart attack was possible and to take some precautions, but he never had.

"It's one of those combinations of things you can't really help," his doctor told him after the heart attack. "I suppose you could have spent your life doing nothing, but then you would probably have died of boredom. Make the most of it, Wilfred. You could live for years if you take care of yourself."

Could, Will thought angrily. *And I might die tomorrow.*

So he thought of Shannon again, her softness, the sweet taste of her lips on his, the disappointment in her eyes when he had told her to go home alone. He had wanted to go with her, as he often did, to sit on her steps and share her quiet company until it was time to sleep, but he couldn't this time. Carol had intruded.

Thinking of Shannon brought only sadness, remembering Carol the old bitterness, so he considered again the boy Robbie, trying to find something that would stop the churning in his mind and allow sleep to claim him. He had to sleep if he was going to function tomorrow. And he had to function. This job was all he had, his only way to live.

Robbie had a face disturbingly like Carol's: a thin, delicate, almost feminine face, and sun streaks in his blondish hair. Robbie, who couldn't swim, didn't like baseball, and wanted to know the names of the butterflies. *In three years, not one of the campers has ever asked me to teach them anything extra. Why this one?*

He wondered for a moment about Robbie's apparent liking for the things of the natural world, the trees, the ferns, the different colored mushrooms with their many forms he had pointed out to them today. Robbie had seemed genuinely interested, and there were so few who were. And Robbie had remembered what he had told them on their earlier trip, quietly asking questions concerning the things Will had pointed out. He was a joy to have along. *If only he didn't look so damn much like Carol.*

But, Will had a long day tomorrow, and he had to have some sleep, so he reluctantly got out of his bunk, took a couple of aspirin, which usually helped, drank a glass of milk which he didn't really want, and went back to bed.

But sleep was still a long time coming.

6. ROBBIE

The mourning cloak rested on the top of a tuft of timothy, slowing fanning its wings in the warming sunshine, the bright yellow and blue bands gleaming in sharp contrast to the blue-black of the under wing. Robbie knelt on the grass watching it and was enthralled.

"I never looked at a butterfly so close before, Mr. Bonneville. I knew they were beautiful but I never saw all of the details before."

"Do you know the names of any butterflies?"

Robbie glanced up at him, sitting on a granite outcropping beside him. "Just tiger swallow-tails and monarchs. The usual ones."

"That's a good start." Mr. Bonneville pulled a small book from his back pocket and handed it to Robbie. "Read that for a while and maybe learn the names of a few more of the common ones. There are a lot of them around here, especially up here in the old fields."

Robbie saw that it was a well-worn paperback called *Golden Nature Guide to Butterflies and Moths.* He sat on the grass and riffled slowly through it, glancing at the pictures. "I didn't know there are so many of them."

"Probably ten thousand kinds in just North America."

Robbie whistled. "Do you know them all, Mr. Bonneville?"

His counselor laughed. "No, of course not, only a couple dozen or so, the most common ones around here. That's why I carry that book around in my pocket. I couldn't possibly remember the seven hundred kinds of butterflies, to say nothing of all the skippers and moths."

Robbie studied the book. "Skippers? What are they?"

"Sort of a halfway between butterflies and moths. They look more like moths, and act more like butterflies, only they sort of skip around through the air. They aren't very bright colored, most of them."

Robbie looked through the guide book until he found them.

His teacher got up slowly. "It's almost time for your swimming lesson."

The Irish setter wandered back from where he had been lying in the shade and poked his nose into Mr. Bonneville's hand.

Robbie glanced sideways at the dog. "What's his name?"

The dog was obviously getting old. A lot of gray showed around his muzzle. Mr. Bonneville smiled at the dog, stroked his head, and scratched behind an ear. "His papers say he is Sir Richard of Galway, but I call him Mick."

"Is he real old? He's sort of gray."

"I'd say about as old as you are, going on twelve."

"He's beautiful."

"You have a dog, Rob?'

"No. We move around too much." He held out his hand and the dog sniffed at it, wagging his tail a little.

"You like Rob, Mick? He doesn't usually like strangers."

Robbie glanced at him, but Mr. Bonneville had turned toward the crest of the hill they had climbed half an hour ago at the start of the free time after lunch. Swimming was the last thing Robbie wanted to do, now or ever. "Do we have to go back down?"

"I'm afraid so. If you're not there, Miss Susan will send out an alarm for you, and that upsets Miss Lucey no end."

Robbie scrambled awkwardly to his feet clutching the guide book.

A mid-sized grayish-brown butterfly with yellow eye-spots on its upper wings flitted past them. Robbie watched it light on a blade of grass. "What's that one, Mr. Bonneville?"

"You have the book."

Robbie kept one eye on the butterfly which was obligingly sitting still, and leafed through the book. He grinned broadly up at his instructor. "This one. A common wood nymph. I never even heard of that one."

"There are lots of them around." Mr. Bonneville started moving away. "Come on, I'll walk back with you as far as my cabin."

Robbie followed reluctantly, still engrossed in the guidebook, but keeping one eye on the path side vegetation for another butterfly. He had noticed there were a great many more of them than he had thought. Once he started looking for them, they seemed to be everywhere.

The next one he saw was another middle sized insect, very dark with reddish bands on the fore wings and bordering the hind wings, and white spots on the tops of the fore wings. He had never seen anything like it. "Mr. Bonneville . . ."

His teacher stopped and turned around.

Robbie pointed at the butterfly still resting on a tall weed.

Mr. Bonneville said patiently, "Look it up, Robbie."

"Oh, sure." It took him a moment to find the red admiral, but when he did, he felt a thrill of satisfaction. "Is it a red admiral, Mr. Bonneville?"

"That is what it looks like. Now, come on, you'll be late and so will I."

"I don't like to swim."

"Why not?"

"I can't float." Admitting it to Mr. Bonneville didn't bother him as much as it usually did. "My mother says that that's nonsense. Everyone can float."

"No, quite a few people can't, but you can learn to swim. You just have to work a little harder at it, and keep moving while you're in the water. What you are probably doing is getting all up tight whenever you go in. You have to relax. Your instructors won't let anything happen to you."

He wondered how Mr. Bonneville knew. "Can I come talk to you after supper when I'm free?"

"I have things to do then."

"Tomorrow then?" He wondered if his eagerness, his hopes, showed in his voice.

"Tomorrow after lunch," Mr. Bonneville said. "For your rest hour."

Robbie smiled at him. "Thanks, Mr. Bonneville."

"Go on now and learn to swim."

Robbie walked toward his cabin by himself. He could see most of the swimmers already on the dock, since they had spent most of their free time in the water. He went into his cabin to change.

A few minutes later he stood on the dock and watched the others swimming. It looked so effortless and looked like fun. He sat on the edge of the dock and dangled his feet in the cool water.

The instructor, Miss Susan, stopped and stood beside him smiling. "Come on now, Robbie, into the water. You don't want to spend your life in the wading pool. Jump in and I'll walk beside you while you try a little."

He slid off the dock into the chest deep water, shocked a moment by the cold. *Relax,* he told himself. *Mr. Bonneville said relax.* Robbie did as Miss Susan had shown him the previous day and felt the panic freezing his limbs. *Relax,* he repeated, forcing his legs to kick a little bit.

"You're doing fine," Miss Susan said.

She was close beside him, and he tentatively stretched out his arm in the long stroke he had been shown. He concentrated on Mr. Bonneville's voice telling him to relax, and found that he was on the farther side of the roped-off non-swimmers' lesson area.

"Great, Robbie," Miss Susan said. "Now let's go back again."

He could hardly believe that he had actually swum all the

way across. He took a deep breath and swam back across with her walking beside him. But his arms were awfully tired.

"That was great, Robbie," she said. "Practice a while now, just like that."

She left him then to rejoin the other swimmers, and he leaned against the dock, very much surprised at himself. He tried, but without Miss Susan walking beside him, he floundered halfway across. He almost gave up then, but he remembered what Mr. Bonneville had said: *You just have to work a little harder at it.*

He went back and tried again.

He managed a bit further the second time, with much floundering, then Miss Susan was beside him again, encouraging him.

"Come back to the dock and try it once more, Robbie."

Her presence gave him some confidence again, and he concentrated on what Mr. Bonneville had told him and the need to relax, and almost made it.

"You'll learn yet, Robbie. Now out, you're turning blue."

He didn't argue with her, but he felt a sort of bubbly elation inside that he had actually swum across the practice area. He had never done it before.

But *they* caught up with him as he was going back up the hill toward his cabin.

"Hey, look, the baby who has to stay in the kiddie pool."

"Can't even swim yet, Robbie?"

"How old are you, Robbie?"

He concentrated on putting one foot in front of the other, pretending he didn't hear them. He had learned ignoring his tormentors sometimes worked.

"Hey, we're talkin' to you."

"Can't you talk neither? Can't swim, can't talk."

He didn't listen to them, kept his eyes focused straight ahead and concentrated on getting safely back to the cabin without losing all of his composure and what ragged dignity he still had.

But they circled him, poking at him, hoping for a reaction from him.

"Hey look, he's cryin'!"

Robbie clenched his teeth tight and kept moving forward.

"Robbie, Robbie, cry-baby!"

They tugged at his clothes and towel. Robbie fought back as best he could, but feebly, and lost his grip on his shirt and the guide book fell onto the ground. He had planned to read it if he could escape the swimming lesson.

Art snatched up the book before Robbie could reach it. "Oh, looky, Robbie likes butterflies."

In desperation and fear for Mr. Bonneville's guide book, Robbie forgot his desire to get away and grabbed for it, hoping it wouldn't be damaged. "Give me that back!"

"Hey, he wants his book."

"You'd better not hurt that book, you . . ."

"Why not, cry baby?"

"What are you going to do if we keep it? Take it away?"

"It's Mr. Bonneville's book, that's why."

That had a momentary sobering effect.

But Corey asked, "How come you've got Mr. Bonneville's book, huh?"

"You steal it, cry-baby?"

"Or have you been out chasing butterflies?"

"Chasing butterflies! Cry-baby Robbie out chasing butterflies."

"That's how come he can't swim."

"'Cause he's out chasing butterflies."

Robbie gave up and stood still, trying not to cry.

A shadow fell across them, silencing the boys instantly. Robbie looked over his shoulder self-consciously at Mr. Bonneville. He dropped his gaze, deeply ashamed of his predicament and his inability to do anything about it.

Mr. Bonneville took his guide book from Art's yielding fingers and handed it to Robbie. He looked at each of the boys in turn and asked a little harshly, "Aren't all of you supposed to study one of the things I pointed out to you today? Have you forgotten that already?"

Robbie was behind the counselor, then escaped silently to his cabin for dry clothes. When he came out, Mr. Bonneville was gone and the boys were coming toward him. He fled toward the wash house.

He hid behind the building, waiting until he saw the others leave for the baseball game that always formed before supper, and then went back to his cabin to wait there alone until the supper bell rang.

He sat on his bunk comparing the pictures of similar butterflies through a mist of tears. What would Mr. Bonneville think of him now? Would he talk to him tomorrow as he had promised, now after Robbie had made such a complete idiot of himself?

He wished, as he had so many times, that he could stand up to them, to all the boys who had tormented him all his life, teased and pushed and stolen his belongings. He thought of his father's comments on it, his urgings that Robbie hit back, blacken their eyes, his bitter sarcasm concerning Robbie's lack of fight.

But he couldn't, couldn't possibly hit anyone, no matter how much they teased, how much his father urged. And now his weakness had cost him the one bright spot he had found in this whole blasted camp! He went out and sat on the steps and watched a big yellow and black butterfly as it flitted past, one he knew was a tiger swallowtail, without even opening the guide book to read about it. He probably wouldn't even get to speak to Mr. Bonneville tomorrow, much less spend his rest hour with him.

He scuffed his way very slowly up the path to the dining hall when the bell finally rang.

7. WILFRED

On the spur of the moment, Will decided to eat supper in the dining hall. He usually avoided the place, disliking the noise, and knowing that the campers at whatever table he chose disliked the formalities his presence imposed on them, but he was curious about Robbie and the boys who had been teasing him. He knew, from his own childhood experience, that the frail boy, the meek and mild one, was picked on as Robbie was, as Will had been. A boy more interested in books than ball games, who was non-athletic, who was maybe considered a little feminine, was suspect. That boy had a rough time unless he had some other kind of strength with which to defend himself.

Will had had physical strength in his arms and shoulders, acquired through long hours of work in the gardens that were his father's business, and he had silenced most of his opposition simply by beating them at arm wrestling. His interest in the natural world had been appreciated by his science teachers, and his high school biology teacher had spent a lot of time trying to influence him in the direction of teaching or research without success. Will had gone into the woods, following an uncle he admired who was a forester. He did not particularly like the business of logging, although he knew that it was essential both to people and to the health of the forest. He spent a lot of time in college studying tree diseases and how to combat them.

Will could see no underlying strength in Robbie. Physically, he was thin, too thin. There was no developing layer of muscle such as Will had had at that age. Nor could he see an inner conviction he was right. Will had gained his beliefs and worldview from his parents. He had their support, assuring him that what he had chosen to be was what was right for him. If he chose to be non-aggressive, then that was his right, even if it sometimes took more courage not to fight than to attack blindly whoever was bothering him.

Robbie appeared to have nothing to support him. His parents had gone off on vacation to some exotic place, leaving Robbie at a camp he detested, apparently with orders to learn skills in which he had no interest and for which he had no aptitude.

The other boys, the ones who had been teasing Robbie, Will knew all too well. The camp was full of them: bored, indulged, naturally aggressive, and full of high spirits. They had always done pretty much as they pleased, always had the odd ball pointed out to them as one to avoid. Be one of the crowd, play ball, look up to Tom Brady and Derek Jeter, or the legends like Larry Bird and Bobby Orr, be like them, real men not sissies. They had all played Little League or Junior Hockey, Pop Warner football, or youth soccer, where the object was to win. The quiet one, the artist, the reader, the non-player, was someone to laugh at.

It annoyed Will, and then he wondered why. *What is Robbie to me? What difference does it make to me if he's having a rotten time? I'm not having a very good time, either.*

But Will knew the reason, in spite of constantly denying it to himself: Robbie's face. The girl he resembled. Will wondered what she looked like now, after twelve years. Was she still the delicate, fragile appearing thing she had been, or had she put on weight? He couldn't really believe that Carol would allow herself to get fat, but she must have matured. He considered, counting back. How old was she when he had last seen her? Twenty-one? Twenty-two? But now she would be in her thirties. He wondered if she was still blonde, or if she had ever been as truly blonde as he remembered her.

Robbie was fair, his blond hair streaked almost white by the sun. He stopped himself there. There was no connection between the two but a similarity of features, something that happened frequently. There are only so many facial types.

Will determinedly put Robbie out of his mind, strode resolutely into the dining hall, and stopped just inside the door. The campers were sorting themselves out into groups around various tables. Miss Lucey had never insisted on a seating plan as such, but each unit had to account for all its members. That counting was now taking place, and Wilfred waited until everyone was duly noted before choosing a table. There were several groups without an adult with them, including the table at which Robbie was standing.

The boy looked up, as if aware he was being watched, and met Will's gaze for a moment before lowering his eyes. His face colored slightly and he turned away.

Sympathizing with the boy's feelings, Will joined a table of girls, pretty girls who giggled when he stopped and asked if he could sit with them. They giggled some more, as they moved their chairs apart, leaving him more than the necessary room. They stood still long enough to mumble the required words before they sat. Will wondered why Miss Lucey still required the saying of grace before meals. The ritual was an empty gesture, he thought, lip service to some past ideal. He said his own prayers, such as they were, in privacy.

He knew from the smells wafting from the kitchen that the main dish was something spicy with tomatoes and there was an undertone of chocolate. Brownies, he knew, were a perennial favorite. The meals were generally good, if they did emphasize nutrition.

From where he sat, Will could see Robbie in profile, and the boy's dejection was painfully obvious. He sat with his head bowed, not attempting to eat, or pass the dishes around the table. The others at his table apparently objected, and

Robbie roused to do as was required of him. Will returned his attention to his own table mates.

Beyond the girl across from him, he saw Shannon watching him, and smiled at her when he caught her eye. Her answering smile was warm, relieving some of the sadness Robbie's situation had caused.

On his right, a dark-haired girl with a curly ponytail said suddenly, "You must like Miss Conley a lot to smile at her like that."

Will smiled at her, too. "Miss Conley is a very nice lady," he said. "And I've known her for quite awhile."

The girl laughed again. The other girls giggled, and she looked away.

"And I saw you just now looking at Mr. Perry over there. Do you like him?"

The girl's cheeks turned pink and the others tittered.

"So, don't talk about anyone else," Will said, not unkindly. "Of course I like Miss Conley. Don't you?"

The girls retreated into a muffled sort of silence, eating their tossed salad and American chop suey with apparent relish, but he noticed them darting sidelong glances at him and then at one another, and heard their stifled giggles.

Their preoccupation gave him a chance to watch Robbie without being obvious, and to watch Shannon, too. Robbie was eating mechanically, ignoring his table mates, and did not appear to be enjoying his meal. Shannon was the center of attention at her table, talking and laughing with the girls sitting there. Although Will could not hear what was being said he could imagine the conversation. Shannon would share stories with them, entertain them.

He liked watching Shannon, hearing her laughter. His heart was there, but he kept glancing at Robbie, and each time he did, he felt a small wave of pity for him. He wondered why since he had seen other unhappy campers, other children who did not enjoy outdoor living, and who had not affected him. Why did this one? *Why Robbie? And it is not his face,* he told himself firmly. *There are a dozen others here who look like that—thin, blond, twelve, and homesick.* Maybe it was just his interest in Wilfred's subject, the one who cared about what Will had to say.

The meal ended with ice cream and frosted brownies and without his arriving at a satisfactory explanation for his feelings. He timed his departure from the dining room to coincide with Shannon's and found himself on the porch at the top of the steps behind Robbie. The boy stood alone, gazing after the others who had run down the path toward their units. He was chewing his lower lip.

Will said, surprising himself, since he had told himself he didn't really care, "Don't give in yet, Robbie."

The boy looked at him, but didn't answer.

"You could stand up to them, if you tried. But, if you don't want to, or figure you can't, just remember it isn't for very long. Whatever methods you usually use for avoiding confrontations will work here as well as they do at home."

The boy stared at him, open mouthed.

"They're bullies, and you are easy to push around. If you didn't push so easily, they wouldn't do it." He shrugged, nodding at Robbie. "Just hang in there, Rob. Camp sessions don't last forever." He stepped around the boy and stood beside Shannon.

Robbie didn't say anything, and Will didn't look back at him as Robbie started down the steps.

"What was all that for?" Shannon asked.

"He has a need." Will followed Shannon down the steps. Ahead of them, Robbie was walking toward the boy's unit. His back seemed to be straighter, his steps a little more sure.

Will smiled slightly and stopped.

Shannon looked back at him. "Will. . ."

"I have to go back to Kaflik and get some things done," he said, "but if you are free a little later to go walking . . ."

"Walking? Haven't you walked enough today?"

Her concern suddenly annoyed him. "I'm going for a walk, just before dark. If you wish to come with me, I would enjoy your company." He followed Robbie down the path.

Shannon caught up to him, and placed her hand on his arm, "Will . . ."

"I'm sorry, Shan. It's all right. I'm just annoyed with the world. Do you have to take part in whatever Miss Lucey has planned for this evening?"

She shook her head, her eyes wide and solemn. He relented. He had to.

"I'll come for you," he said, and because of the concern in her eyes, he added, "I had a very easy day today, Shan. And you know that walking is what I am supposed to do."

"I'm only afraid you'll overdo."

He put his hand on hers where it rested on his arm and squeezed lightly. "In a little while," he promised . "I have to make sure everything is set for a craft project we are doing tomorrow. I won't be very long."

Robbie was nowhere in sight when he walked through the boy's unit to Kaflik. Wilfred breathed a small measure of relief and went into the unit house to finish his day's reports and prepare for the next day's activities. He looked at the accumulation on his desk, papers he needed to deal with, and was suddenly terribly tired. Not physically tired. He used his body so carefully, it rarely felt tired. Mentally, spiritually tired. Emotionally drained. And he did not know why.

Why had he been so sharp with Shannon? He had no desire to hurt her or annoy her, so why had he risked losing her company tonight? Why should her concern for his health annoy him now, when she had been concerned about him for well over a year?

He got up from his messy desk, stacked his books and notes, partially straightened out the piles of papers, turned out the lights, and went out onto the porch, determined to put all of the day's problems and frustrations out of his mind until tomorrow. He almost stepped on the boy sitting in the shadows.

"I'm sorry, Mr. Bonneville," Robbie said quickly, getting up and backing away from him.

Will caught his arm and pulled him into the fading light where he could see him. "What are you doing here?" he asked, with more annoyance than he felt.

Robbie's chin quivered a bit, but he kept his gaze steady on Will's. "Hiding," he said. "I didn't think anyone would come over here."

"And why hide?"

"It's easier."

Will let go of his arm, sighed deeply, and pointed to the steps. "Sit down."

Robbie sat quickly, as close to one of the railings as he could get, and drew his knees up under his chin.

Will sat on the other side, leaving a space between them. "All right," he said, trying to hide his weariness. "Talk about it."

"About what?"

"Whatever's bothering you."

Robbie peered into the gathering dusk. "About them, Mr. Bonneville?"

"Who's them?"

Robbie didn't answer. He glanced once in Will's direction, and then back toward the cabins.

"The boys in your cabin, you mean? The way they tease you?"

Robbie nodded.

"Why, really, did you come over here to hide? You knew I was here. And I had told you that I would be too busy to talk to you."

"They knew you were here, too," Robbie said so softly that Will almost didn't hear him.

"So you figured you'd be safe for awhile."

Robbie didn't answer.

Will released a long breath, got control of himself, and mentally settled down for a siege. "How is it at home, Rob?" he asked.

"All right. I get along, mostly."

"You have any brothers or sisters?"

"No." He added, as if it were an afterthought, "Not at home."

"Older? Away from home?"

"They're my father's," Robbie said. "A little older than me. They live down south somewhere. I've only seen them once."

Wilfred digested that silently.

"My parents both work," Robbie said. "My father travels quite a bit."

"Who looks out for you?"

"Nobody, any more. I mean, Mom comes home for supper and stuff."

"You mean you used to have a sitter, and now you don't?"

Robbie nodded. "They said I'm too old for a sitter."

Will thought he was much too young and vulnerable to be without someone. "What do you do for fun?"

"Fun?"

"Yeah. Run hundred yard dashes, read books, fly kites, or beat everybody else at marbles?"

"Oh," Robbie said. "I read a lot, belong to the Science Club at school. I won a checkers tournament once. I . . ." He stopped, looking down at his hands.

Will wondered what else he had been going to say. "What do you do in gym class?"

"I hate gym class."

"All of it? Isn't there anything you like to do?"

Robbie glanced at him, then quickly away. But Will had seen the agony there. "I liked gymnastics, once," Robbie said, "but my parents didn't approve of it."

"Why?" He could see where Robbie might be well suited to acrobatics. And it would strengthen his arms.

Robbie whispered, "They said it was a girls' sport."

Will didn't answer that one. He wondered what Robbie's father looked like.

Robbie sat still, not offering any more information.

"And you can't stand baseball," Will said.

Robbie shook his head.

"And your father is a baseball nut."

"Football."

"Television kind?"

"He played in high school and college some."

Wilfred had a better idea what Robbie's father looked like. Robbie would never have that kind of build. He said a small thank-you to whatever powers that be for his own father's ideas along that line. His father had been a powerful man.

"Do you understand football?"

"No. I don't even like to watch it. It's too rough, people get hurt. I . . . I'd rather go to a baseball game with him."

Will decided that 'him' meant Robbie's father and changed his question. "What is your favorite subject?"

"Science. Math isn't too bad."

Will had a sudden vision of himself at twelve, the quiet studious kind, not liking ball games, preferring to sit on the side lines with a good book. His father had given him a telescope and opened up another whole world. He asked, "Do you like biology?"

"Biology?"

"Trees and plants. All living things."

"Oh. Yeah. Like butterflies." Robbie smiled for the first time.

Will asked, mostly out of personal curiosity, "Do you get along with your parents?"

"Of course!"

Robbie's answer had been too quick, too loud, too defensive, and Will felt sorry for him again. He asked, surprising himself that he did so, "And what did they tell you to get out of Camp Rocky Point?"

Robbie laughed, dully and without mirth. "I have to learn to swim and to play baseball. Get to know some guys." He added, when his voice broke a little, "I did like you told me, Mr. Bonneville, and I swam across the beginners' pool, almost."

"Alone?"

"Miss Susan was walking with me. But I was swimming."

"Good for you. Just keep practicing. It's a good thing to know."

Robbie turned toward the lake, shining gold and red in the sunset beyond the cabins. "I'd like to go out in a boat, but they won't take the non-swimmers like me."

"Even with a life jacket?"

Robbie shook his head. "It's an incentive, they call it. You have to earn your way out there."

"Um." That rule was one of many that he disagreed with but could not change.

A whistle suddenly blew shrilly three times from beyond the row of cabins. Robbie looked up, and Will got slowly to his feet, wondering why an alarm had been blown.

A voice reached them, calling sharply, "Robbie! Robert Sullivan!"

Robbie turned a frightened face toward Will.

"Come along," Will said. "You have to go face the music for not being where you're supposed to be when you're supposed to be there."

Robbie followed him silently.

They rounded the nearest cabin and found a group in the center of the boy's unit. Will pulled Robbie closer beside him, holding his arm, half afraid the boy would bolt.

Perry was in charge, preparing to send searchers out in a prearranged pattern. He did not look pleased.

Will said, "Perry!" without raising his voice particularly.

The whole group turned and looked at them.

Wilfred felt Robbie move back, trying to hide within himself. He tightened his grip a little, keeping the boy firmly in front of him. "He was only talking to me by the unit house."

Perry came toward them, scowling. "Well, he's supposed to let somebody know."

Robbie looked at his feet. "I didn't see anybody to tell. You were all over by the ball field."

"Well," Perry said, "haven't you anything else to say?"

"I'm sorry."

"You should be, getting the camp all in an uproar."

"You blew the whistle a full two minutes ago," Will said mildly, "and he came as soon as you called. What more do you want?"

Perry apparently couldn't argue with that. He turned away. "Well, he shouldn't have gone over there without telling somebody where he was going."

"True." Will let go of Robbie's arm. "Go on, boy, and do whatever it is you are supposed to be doing."

Robbie glanced at him over his shoulder. "Thanks. Loads." He trudged ed away toward his cabin.

Will thought of his own cabin, and headed that way. Shannon would be waiting for him, along with the peace and quiet he really needed.

8. SHANNON

Shannon Conley sat on her cabin steps with a cup of tea enjoying the evening coolness while she unwound from her day and waited for Will to join her. This was the best part of her day, and just thinking about it sometimes got her through a seemingly endless parade of banged knees, scraped elbows, little girls' hurt feelings, and upset stomachs she suspected were caused more by those hurt feelings than an over indulgence in dessert.

She debated for a moment if she should walk across the top of the hill to Will's cabin, but decided not to. He would expect to find her here, and she would wait for him. She heard the three blasts of the signal whistle, not realizing for a moment what it meant, that there was a problem somewhere, and when she did she panicked. *Will! He's had a heart attack and collapsed!* She dropped her cup beside her and started down the path, not quite running, her growing fear both turning her knees to jelly and spurring her on. *Please, let him be okay.* She met him in the middle of the hill and almost collapsed in his arms.

"Oh, Will, the alarm scared me. I thought maybe you . . ."

He laughed at her, and held her tight for a moment, close but not touching. "It was just Robbie," he said, "talking to me instead of playing ball with everyone else, and Perry over reacted."

She tried to laugh, but she was still out of breath and trying to quash her fear.

"Silly girl," he said, releasing his hold on her and steering her around to walk up the hill again. "If it had been me they would have quietly sent somebody for you, not roused the whole camp."

She should have known that. She said, still shaking inside, "Of course, I didn't think." She tried to laugh but couldn't. "I guess I overreacted, too."

She put her hand in his and determined, firmly, that she would say or do nothing tonight to upset him. But she would much rather have his arms around her.

He tightened his hold on her hand and drew her closer. She matched her steps with his slower ones and said nothing. "I have a brother named Edward," he said, his gaze on the path ahead of them. "He's a little younger than I am, but quite a bit bigger. He's thought for quite awhile that he has to take care of me. In fact, he started thinking that way when he was about ten."

Shannon wondered what that had to do with her. Her sisters had long ago left her to her own devices. "You've never mentioned your family before."

"There's just me and Ed now." He paused, still not looking at her. "You've been reminding me of him lately, thinking that I can't take care of myself."

"I'm just . . . concerned." She did not want to say *in love with you and I worry about you*, although that is what she meant. She added, even though she didn't mean it, "And just as a nurse, of course. That's how I am."

"And I'm grateful, Shan, really, but I can take care of myself. I've been doing it for quite some time now . If that had been me in trouble back there, no one would have blown the whistle. Someone would have come for you, if they did anything."

"Of course they'd do something." But she knew he was right. No one would have upset the children.

"Maybe." He added, as if an afterthought, "If something ever does happen to me, get in touch with Ed, will you? His address is there in the cabin somewhere with my things."

The thought was chilling, something she didn't want to think about, but she managed to say, "Of course," quite steadily.

"And now stop moping around about my health, about which you can do nothing, and enjoy the evening."

It was a nice evening, pleasantly cool, with breeze enough to discourage the mosquitoes, clear with a bright moon coming up across the lake. She hoped that he was not planning on a long walk even at his usual rambling gait. "Why did they think Robbie was lost?"

"He was hiding over by Kaflick from his unpleasant cabin-mates and no one knew where he'd gotten off to. Perry was making one his checks to be sure everyone had come in from washing up or something."

"I've never seen you take so much interest in one of the campers before. Why Robbie?"

"I never found an interesting one before. Maybe I should say interested. Rob likes what I teach."

"The first one? I can't believe that."

"Oh, there've been a few, usually girls, but Rob has apparently studied some before and knows a lot." He turned off the path they were following, and headed for the old barn. Relieved at this decision, that he planned to just relax and not climb to the top of the hill, she asked, "Robbie likes your nature talks?"

"He comes after hours asking for more. With intelligent questions."

She couldn't think of any answer to that except, *Of course he does, so would I,* and that didn't seem the proper thing to say.

Will didn't say anything more, so she strolled beside him in silence, enjoying the quiet. From somewhere beyond the trees in front of them she could hear singing from the girls' unit, some kind of spiritual accompanied by a guitar, and from behind them occasional laughter or a shout from the boys' cabins. The sounds were not unpleasant, and as they were muted, not at all distracting from the other night sounds around them: the deep-throated galumph of a bullfrog; the tentative call of an owl; clicking of insects.

The barn was in front of them, looming large in the dusk. They rounded it going to the far corner by the door, where there was a bank to sit on.

He stopped suddenly. "Hey, the door's open."

He let go of her hand, tugged the door open a little further, and peered inside. "Is anybody in there?"

She looked over his shoulder, but the interior of the barn was almost total blackness.

Wilfred straightened up and closed the door, turning the wooden bar lock securely. "Kids," he said. "They know this place is off limits but some of them just can't resist. Challenge of it, I suppose."

"Couldn't it open by itself? The wind, maybe?"

"Not possible." He sat down and leaned back against the side of the building. "That door stopper turns too hard to jiggle loose."

She settled herself beside him, close, but not quite touching him. "And why is it so terrible if the kids do come up here?"

"There's a lot of junk in there. The stairs aren't all that safe, no hand rails, and the whole place is a fire trap. I never did get it properly cleaned out, you know."

"The other counselors could have done it before camp opened, they should have. It wouldn't have hurt them any or taken them very long."

"It was my job, and I had all spring to get it done."

She didn't want to argue with him, so she leaned back and looked up at the sky. The stars were beginning to appear. She wished silently on the first one she saw. *Keep him well, make him happy, make him mine . . .*

He clasped his hands around his drawn-up knee, gazing down the hill at the cabins below them, but didn't say anything.

She watched him without speaking, wondering what he was thinking, wishing she could see his face clearly. But she knew he preferred she not speak, so she sat still, listening for whatever he was hearing, and waited for him to break the silence. She heard the crickets in the grass, and the sleepy twitterings of a bird. The passing traffic on the state highway reminded her the camp was not really isolated from the community. She waited, as she had learned to wait.

When Will did speak, he surprised her. "I hadn't thought about Ed for a long time. He must be thinking about me."

"Were you close to him?"

He angled his head toward her. "Maybe. In a way. We got along all right."

"You don't see him very often? He lives a long way away?"

"Not too far. He came when . . . I was in the hospital, and took care of things for me. He came out here once last winter to see how I was making out and go out to dinner, catch up on family and such. I haven't seen him since. I guess he didn't see any need."

She wondered at his apparent reluctance to talk about his brother, but did not ask any more questions. It was so easy to make him withdraw into himself and say nothing at all. She didn't want to talk about Robbie any more, either, so she again sat and waited for him to speak, watching his face which was barely visible in the growing dark.

But he surprised her again. "Ed's a lot like our father was. Looks like him, thinks like him. I'm like some other branch of the family, some relative of my mother's, she said once. It caused a few problems."

She could see where that could be. Her choice of a nursing career had not been her mother's preference. Shannon was supposed to go into law or something with more prestige. "Everybody's a little different. My sister Abby and I don't agree very often about anything."

He turned toward her, but she couldn't see his face. "We all knew that. No one expected me to be like Ed, or vice-versa. He's him, and I'm me."

She started to ask what had caused problems then, but he said, "That's the trouble Robbie Sullivan is having right now. He's the odd one. At home."

This was safe ground, so she asked, "He talked about home to you?"

"A little. The rest I could surmise because I was like that, the quiet one who didn't like ball games." He paused a moment his face toward the lake where she could see the last colors of the sunset fading away behind the trees. "His folks sent him here to be made over into the athletic type while they went off on vacation. At least my folks never did that to me."

She remembered Robbie's sad, thin, almost fragile appearing face and his big eyes.

"He has a lot of potential they apparently don't see," Will said. "He doesn't want to be what they think he should be, what they want." He took her hand. "I did not come all the way up here with you to talk about Robbie. Or about Edward."

She squeezed his fingers, but didn't say anything.

"I told you about Carol the other day, and why I can't get involved like that again."

"You only told me that you had been unhappily married. You gave me no reason why you can't marry again, only your health, which doesn't count. At least not with me."

"My health has to count. You know that I may have very little time left."

"I'd like to make that time good, Will. I love you."

"Why?" he asked. "She couldn't find anything to love. How can you? I'm a lot less man now than I was then."

"Because you are a good man, Will." She tried to blink away the tears in her eyes. She wanted to put both arms around him and hold him, reassure him, love him. "Call it chemistry," she said, "or call it biology, I don't know. I only know I do. I want to take care of you, to keep you safe."

"Is that reason enough to want to throw your life away?"

"I don't think I'd be throwing it away."

He didn't answer, and she wondered again what Carol had done to him to leave him so bitter.

She said softly, taking a chance, "Will, I'm not Carol. This is me, Shannon Conley, and we are different."

She thought he was going to withdraw, take his hand from hers, retreat into himself again, but he didn't.

"I know, Shan. It's the only thing that keeps me here. I know that you couldn't be like that. You're an honest person." She heard him take a deep shuddering breath. "And much too young."

His fingers had tightened around hers for an instant, alerting her. "Will, are you in pain?"

"It comes and goes."

"Don't get yourself upset. Please, relax a little." She struggled to keep her anxiety out of her voice, to stay calm, professional as he wanted her.

He let go of her hand. "Come here, closer."

She scooted over a little, and he put his arm around her. "What do I know about you?" he asked. "You have two sisters. Fern is older, and Abby is younger. You graduated from a teaching hospital in upstate New York. You came here to hide from a broken engagement. You are twenty-seven years old and figure you are going to die an old maid. You get letters once in awhile from your mother and from Fern. In the winter you have an efficiency apartment and work in the emergency clinic connected with the hospital. Right?"

"Partly. I don't consider myself an old maid."

"Not old," he agreed. "Young and pretty with so much more ahead of you than I can offer."

She rested her face against his chest and didn't answer.

"You have to think about that," he said urgently. "You have so much life ahead of you, and I don't."

"I want to spend as much of it as possible with you."

His arm tightened around her. When he spoke again, his voice was strained. "God, Shan, you make it hard." He released her.

Even in the dark she could see the pain on his face, and it hurt her. She felt his pain in her own chest, but she could not speak. His fingers tightened again, biting into her arms.

"Will," she whispered urgently, "relax. The spasm will ease a little bit."

His fingers loosened slowly, and he leaned against her, resting his head on her shoulder.

She steadied him with her hands. "I'm sorry. Every time I talk to you I upset you. Do you need your pills?"

"No. No, I'm all right now."

"You're sure?"

He nodded, not speaking, and she held him a little tighter, wishing there was something she could do to ease the pain, the excruciating spasms, for him.

"Sometimes it is almost more than I can stand. It seems so useless to keep going."

"Oh, Will, no. There is always reason to go on." A chill crept along her spine, and her arms tightened a little convulsively.

He laughed. "Don't worry, Shan. I'm too much of a coward to do anything like that. I never could do anything about anything or anybody who was bothering me."

She considered his fight against the pain, his working here in spite of it. "You're not a coward."

"Ed always said I was." He straightened and disengaged her hands from his arms so he could hold them. "He fought most of my battles for me, all those I couldn't. Or wouldn't."

She couldn't frame a reply. She was still shaking inside and trying to conceal it from him.

He cupped his fingers around her face. When he kissed her lightly on the cheek she knew that he found it wet with tears. He said softly, "God, I can't help it, but I love you."

"Will . . ."

He kissed her gently, barely touching her lips with his, and held her close. "But it can't ever be."

She did not try to control her tears.

9. ROBBIE

Robbie Sullivan rummaged through his footlocker, disrupting the precise order in which he had been told to keep all of his belongings and creating a jumbled mess. What he wanted, of course, was tucked into the last corner in which he searched. There was no time to straighten it out, so he smoothed the top a little and slammed the cover down, belatedly remembering to lock it, and put the key chain around his neck. He grabbed the disposable camera he had retrieved and ran to where his unit was gathering for a hike up the long hill behind the camp.

Every camper had been given a camera when they arrived and tonight they were supposed to turn them in, all the shots taken, so they could be developed in town. *Turn them in,* they were told, *or no supper, or at least no dessert.* He wondered if that were so and decided it wasn't, since they had to be fed, but he knew his mother was expecting pictures. He had taken very few because he had seen little he wanted to photograph, so today he had to catch up.

The others in the unit were there ahead of him, forming the usual straggling line, and he was dismayed to find that another counselor, Mr. Dan, was going with them. It wasn't that he disliked Mr. Dan, but he was overwhelmed by him. Dan played basketball at some college, and he towered over the campers, and over Mr. Bonneville as well. And he had a loud voice and joked a lot.

Robbie joined the group as inconspicuously as possible. Mr. Bonneville said, "We're all here, let's go."

Robbie joined the line near the end. He wasn't where he wanted to be, but it was a place where he wouldn't be noticed. The boys were strung out along the path, divided into twos and threes. They stopped frequently as Mr. Bonneville pointed out bits of nature, an oddly shaped rock formation, a growth on a tree. Robbie worked his way forward, passing only one person or group each time they stopped. When they reached the top of the hill, Robbie was in the place he wanted to be: directly behind Mr. Bonneville where he could hear everything. Mr. Dan was at the back of the group, where he said, grinning maliciously, he could make sure there were no stragglers or deserters.

At the high point of the hill, out of sight of the camp and lake, there was a wide granite ledge, mostly shady and just right for sitting. Mr. Bonneville called his first halt.

"Take five," he said, and settled himself on the ledge.

Robbie sat nearby and took the camera out of his pocket. He focused it on his leader, centering his face in the window, and said, "Mr. Bonneville?"

The counselor looked up, and Robbie took his picture, and just to be sure he had a good one, he snapped another. That was the only picture he really wanted.

Mr. Bonneville smiled at him, but said nothing, and turned away, apparently to watch the antics of a group of boys farther down the hill.

Robbie didn't know what else to do, what else to photograph, and he had half the exposures left.

A hand lightly touched his shoulder, and he turned. His gaze followed Mr. Bonneville's pointing finger to a clump of yellow-flowering weeds behind them. The butterfly resting there was of medium size, brown with a wide orange band along outer edge of the wings. Robbie focused his camera on it and snapped the picture before it moved. "What kind is it? I didn't bring the book." He wished now that he had remembered it. "I don't remember seeing that one."

The butterfly moved to a clump of grass and then fluttered away.

"That's a peculiar one," Mr. Bonneville said. "A male Diana. The female has blue on it instead of orange."

"How come?" Robbie asked.

"Who knows? One of those odd things." Mr. Bonneville straightened. "Okay, you guys, let's get in line. Sam, pick up that gum wrapper."

The leader stood beside Robbie, watching as the group reorganized, and when Robbie joined the line again, he was one step behind him.

Their path followed the crest of the hill for a dozen yards in the sunshine then dipped into a shallow, tree-shaded valley. They stopped at the edge of a small brook splashing its way over a series of low, wide ledges to form a chain of little pools between the rocks. Birch and maple trees overhung the water, dappling the sunlight, which touched the water with dancing sparkles. Dark green moss formed a deep carpet along the edges of the brook, and several small frogs plopped into a pool as the boys approached. Robbie stood still, enjoying the quiet beauty of the spot, and was distinctly irritated when two stones landed in one of the pools. He glanced sideways at his leader and saw a trace of annoyance on his face, too, before he hid it and asked if anyone remembered the names of the trees along the brook.

Several trees were named by two or three different voices, most of them obvious guesses. Robbie said softly, not much more than a whisper, "The white ones are paper birches, and the raggedy-looking one over on the other side is a yellow birch, and the big one behind us with the gray bark is a beech. Most of the others are maples."

There was complete silence for a long moment, then a voice in back said in mock awe, "Gee, a professor."

"He's right, you know," Mr. Bonneville said, a strange note in his voice that Robbie could not identify. "At least someone around here does his homework." He turned away from the brook, and the group followed him along the path, around the edge of the hill and into the sunshine again on top.

Robbie shuffled silently behind him, wishing he had kept his knowledge to himself, hadn't tried to show off a little and impress Mr. Bonneville. He had recognized the e mocking voice of his bunk-mate Corey , and Corey was the acknowledged head of the whole group, usually the leader of the teasing. Robbie had visions of the coming evening and shuddered. *Why didn't I just keep my mouth shut?*

The sun was pleasantly warm on his head, calming his nerves. The grass and field flowers along the path smelled so enticing he wanted to lie down among them and watch the clouds move and not have to do anything. *Not have to think about anything.* That thought was so enjoyable, he did not pay attention to where they were walking until their Mr. Bonneville said suddenly, "Okay, guys, stop for a minute."

Robbie glanced around, chose an outcropping of gray rock somewhat to the side of the others as his place, and sat there, hoping to stay unnoticed. Mr. Bonneville sat beside him, however, rested his arms on his knees and looked out over the valley below them.

Robbie didn't say anything. He kept his back toward his counselor, but he was very conscious of Mr. Bonneville's presence. He wished they were alone so he could talk to him, really talk to him, but he could not talk here, with all the other people around. Especially his cabin-mates.

Mr. Bonneville's attention was apparently focused down the hill, where the far side of Pleasant Pond was just visible. Robbie could see no sign of Camp Rocky Point, but knew it must lie almost directly below them.

"All right, Rob," Mr. Bonneville said quietly, "where did you learn your trees? We haven't discussed those you named, no beech, and no yellow birch since they aren't all that common around here."

Robbie was too startled to answer for a moment. He hadn't expected to be spoken to. "It was a merit badge. Forestry. The first one I earned."

"If you're a Boy Scout, why are you here instead of at a Boy Scout camp?"

"I don't know. I guess my folks thought this one was better. Or something like that."

"Don't they approve of Boy Scouting?"

"Nobody objects. Except to the things I choose to get my merit badges in."

"Butterflies and basket weaving?"

That was too close to the truth for Robbie to talk about. He didn't answer.

"It's an odd Boy Scout who doesn't like camping. Isn't that one of the objectives?"

"The camping part is all right." In fact, he would probably enjoy it with the right people. It was people like his cabin-mates that made it so bad. He didn't say so, however.

"But not this camp." Mr. Bonneville got up slowly.

Robbie noticed for the first time how slowly and carefully his leader moved. It surprised him and he wondered why, if there was something wrong with his leader, some medical problem, but he dismissed the thought. Robbie also stood, but stayed where he was until the line formed again, wanting this time to stay toward the end, invisible and away from comment and further problems.

But Mr. Bonneville's hand was on his shoulder, urging him forward, keeping Robbie beside him. Robbie went, not wanting to refuse and cause more comment, really wanting to be with the only person in the whole damned camp he could care about, but thinking about what his cabin-mates would say about it later made him ill. There were always consequences that were so hard to deal with.

Mr. Bonneville let go of Robbie's arm almost as soon as they had started on again, and paid no more attention to him, as they proceeded slowly, but steadily along the side of the hill, and then turned back, angling down as the path turned toward the camp. Mr. Bonneville did not speak to him until they were in the trees again, talking instead as he always did to the group as a whole about the things around them. He had pointed out some odd-shaped, evil looking, dark brown mushrooms noting that they were quite poisonous, several kinds of greenish lichens on an old stump, a crow sitting on a post, and a hawk circling high above them, naming it a red-tailed.

"There are lots of things to see if you take time to look," the counselor said. "That's an added benefit to the exercise."

Robbie relaxed a little, began to enjoy the outing again, and they entered another stretch of woodland.

"Now," Mr. Bonneville said, quite pointedly to Robbie, but not very loudly, "I want to check out this instructor you had in forestry."

Robbie glanced at him, surprised at his rather sharp tone, but Mr. Bonneville was smiling as usual. "There are a couple of trees along here that are a little different from your birch and maple, which everybody should know." He glanced at the others, then at the tree beside him. "I want to see if you really earned that badge."

Robbie's stomach tightened painfully. He knew he had studied his trees well, and remembered them, but his badge instructor had been a lot different from Mr. Bonneville, just stressing the identifying characteristics. He didn't want to appear stupid now, and he didn't want his counselor thinking he hadn't really earned his badge. What Mr. Bonneville thought about him had suddenly become important, and what the other boys thought was of no importance at all. He still said nothing. His mouth was too dry.

The tree Mr. Bonneville pointed out to him was slender, not much bigger around than his arm, tall in proportion to its thickness. Robbie could not see its leaves, but the bark was distinctive, greenish with white stripes. He felt a vast surge of relief. "Moosewood," he said. "Striped maple."

The counselor smiled at him, and then pointed out the tree's characteristics to the other boys. They continued along the path. The next shrub Mr. Bonneville indicated was one of the oddest Robbie had encountered. His badge counselor had made much of it because it had leaves in three shapes, some single ovals, some three-lobed, and some mitten-shaped. When Mr. Bonneville finished talking about it, he asked Robbie to name it.

"Sassafras."

"Only one more, Rob, and I'll believe you had a half-decent badge counselor."

The path wound around clumps of trees and Mr. Bonneville continued his talk about plant succession, interdependence of plants and animals, and the general ecology of the forest, until they came to the far side of the wooded area and were again at the edge of the open field.

Mr. Bonneville stopped and pointed to a large tree. "This is another of our native species most people forget about. You know this one, Rob?"

The tree above him had dark, deeply furrowed bark and big heart shaped leaves. He knew he had read about it, seen the pictures, but its name escaped him.

Mr. Bonneville turned away, speaking to the group. "The flowers are very popular with bees and make a nice flavored honey. The wood is used in cabinet making." He was again looking at Robbie, who was still staring into the tree, trying to remember the name. His mind was a complete blank.

A voice, probably Art's said, "Gee, the professor can't remember."

Another answered, "You mean there's one he doesn't know?"

Robbie knew his face was turning red. He suddenly felt sick to his stomach and fought to control it.

"Did you ever see a tree like this one before?" Mr. Bonneville asked.

"Yes."

He waited a long minute during which Robbie's mind stayed distressingly empty. "I can't remember," he said finally.

Mr. Bonneville turned away. "The tree," he said, "is a basswood."

They left the trees for the heat of the field again. Robbie waited until the whole group was past him before he moved. He scuffed along alone at the end of the line, just ahead of Mr. Dan, no longer caring what Mr. Bonneville had to say. He had blown his chance, and he did not expect another one. He knew he was going to be sick. When he was upset, he was always sick and there was little he could do about it

The narrow, rutted path they were following turned sharply around a high out-jutting granite ledge. The track was somewhat eroded on the lower side, with loose gravel on the sharpest part of the turn, and Robbie, in his sadness, did not notice and stepped too close to the edge of the path, His foot landed among the small stones. He turned his ankle, lost his balance, and fell hard on his left hip. He tried to catch himself as he fell, but he was over the edge of the steep slope. He rolled over several times and stopped against a dense clump of prickly juniper bushes.

He banged his chest hard as he fell and was still trying to catch his breath and control his stomach when he heard an angry buzzing. Then came the hot agonizing stings on his face, the back of his neck, and exposed parts of his arms. He screamed and fought against the angry swarm of hornets, but he was too entangled in the prickly clinging juniper bushes and could not escape.

He heard yelling and big hands pulled him roughly from the entangling bush, away from the damaged nest, and swept aside the hornets still clinging to him. Mr. Dan moved him farther from the bush, safely away from the angry insects.

And then other, gentler hands touched him, removed more of the yellow jackets from his neck but kept him lying where Mr. Dan had put him.

"Are you hurt any place besides the stings?" Mr. Bonneville asked.

Robbie controlled his roiling stomach with an effort. "I think my ankle."

"You got anything for those stings?" Mr. Dan asked. "He's swelling up bad. All over."

"You can get down to the infirmary as fast as I can do anything."

The other boys were ringing them, watching wide-eyed but not crowding too close. Robbie lost control of his queasy stomach. "I'm going to be sick." It was the final indignity, and even Mr. Bonneville's hands holding him steady while he lost his dinner did little to help. He sat on the hard ground, shaking and clammy, and wished he was dead.

"Dan, get out that cell phone of yours and call down to Miss Conley quick," Mr. Bonneville said calmly. "He's taken a lot of poison, and I don't know how allergic he might be. Get the camp Jeep, and we'll be coming as fast as we can to meet you."

Dan fished his phone out of his pocket, turned and sprinted up the hill while punching in the numbers.

"I don't think I'm allergic." Robbie was still shaking, still sweating, still cold and clammy, still totally annoyed with himself.

Mr. Bonneville helped him onto his feet and held him steady. "Can you walk?"

Robbie put his left foot down experimentally. The pain was intense. He shook his head.

Mr. Bonneville put one arm around Robbie's shoulders and started helping him up the slope, moving slowly and half-carrying him, letting Robbie use his good foot. When they reached the top they stopped and Mr. Bonneville turned to the boys still crowding around, "Okay, all the rest of you, get back to camp as fast as you can and tell Mr. Perry what happened. I'll take Robbie along to Miss Conley." When they didn't move, he said, "Robbie will be all right. Move along. Now."

They moved, slowly at first, along the path, glancing back, and then ran when they reached the point where they could see the camp.

Robbie watched them go, glad they were gone, and wondered for a moment what would happen to him now, would they take him to the hospital, or would Miss Conley take care of him here? Would they call his parents and interrupt their trip? How mad would his mother be? He didn't want to go anywhere, but he was really too sick to care.

10. SHANNON

"You're not half as bad off as we first thought, Robbie," Shannon said with considerably more confidence than she felt. "The doctor only counted seventeen stings. That's a lot more than I ever had at one time. Thank goodness."

The boy was lying on a cot in the inner room of the main lodge, a cramped space they euphemistically called an infirmary. It was really not much more than a first-aid station, but it did have a separate entrance from a small porch. Real emergencies were to be handled somewhere else. Robbie was pasty white, still felt a little clammy when she put her hand on his forehead, and he had been sick to his stomach again. The angry swollen red marks of the stings were fading.

"So," she told him cheerfully, "just make yourself as comfortable as you can."

He regarded her somberly and didn't answer.

She tried again. "That must have really hurt."

"I guess." His voice was soft, hesitant.

She smiled at him. "Just lie still, Robbie. The doctor said you will be all right in spite of the number of stings." She tucked the thick blue camp blanket a little tighter around him. "Are you sure you've never had a reaction to a hornet sting?"

"I'm sure."

"Did you ever get stung more than once?"

"Twice once."

She sat in a chair beside him, still concerned about his paleness, although his pulse and blood pressure were normal, and his temperature had not gone up. "How do you feel now?"

"Better."

He sounded very far away, and she wondered if he ever volunteered any information. He had not been very communicative with the doctor in the emergency room, either, barely answering questions. She knew a report had been sent to his parents, but didn't know if there had been a response. It was probably too soon if they were in Bermuda.

"Are you still sick to your stomach?" she asked.

"No."

She thought his face flushed a little and put her hand on his forehead. "Do you feel up to telling me how it happened? Surely there isn't a hornets' nest anywhere near the hiking trail."

Dan had given her a hurried explanation, but it had not been very clear. And he had not stayed once he had given it, either, leaving her to take the Jeep up the hill to meet Will and Robbie. Dan had to go and see that the other hikers were all back at their unit and okay, he'd said, and had left running. She thought he was scared and was surprised. Will had seen Robbie comfortably settled into the Jeep, and she had taken him to the emergency room while Will went to report to Miss Lucey.

"I'll keep her calm," he promised. "And out of your hair."

"I slipped," Robbie said. "I stepped on a loose stone, fell down and rolled down the hill and into some bushes where the hornets were."

"Oh." She knew he had twisted his ankle, but not badly. The emergency room doctor had wrapped it in an Ace bandage, advised applying ice packs, and told Robbie to stay off it for the rest of the day and take it easy tomorrow. His other injuries were a collection of minor scrapes and bruises that had been washed and covered with an antibiotic cream.

Robbie asked, "Did I lose my camera? If I did, my mother—"

"Were you carrying it when you fell? I haven't seen it."

He closed his eyes and looked ill again.

"I'm sure someone will go back and look for it for you."

"It was in my pocket. My mother wanted some pictures."

"What did you take pictures of?" *Maybe if he talks he'll feel better.*

"My cabin-mates, some neat butterflies, stuff like that. And Mr. Bonneville. He didn't know I was going to take it."

"That is usually the best way to get good pictures of people."

She heard footsteps on the porch, the screen door opening and closing softly. Shannon got up to see who it was and met Will in the outer office.

He greeted her with his gentle smile and a light squeeze on the upper arm. "How's our young friend?"

"He seems to be all right. The doctor says he'll be fine."

Will let go of her arm and walked into the room where Robbie was lying. She stopped in the doorway and watched him looking down at Robbie.

"I found your camera," Will said. "It looks okay. I turned it in to the office for you. You'll have your prints tomorrow like everyone else. I also did something about the yellow jackets, sort of discouraged them a bit."

Robbie smiled thinly at him. "Thank you."

"You don't look much worse for the wear. How do you feel?"

"Okay." She could see Robbie's face and the life that had suddenly returned almost normal color in his cheeks. She looked at Will and was again surprised. She thought, *they really like each other.*

"You weren't sick up there just because of the hornet stings." Will did not put it as a question but stated it as a fact.

Robbie turned his head away. "No."

Will laughed. "You won't forget the basswood tree again."

She saw Robbie catch his lower lip in his teeth and wondered what had happened. "A basswood tree? Will, what do you do to your students?"

"Beat them unmercifully when they don't know the right answers."

Robbie smiled but didn't say anything.

"Rob knew all the right answers but one, which was a heck of a lot more than anyone else knew."

Robbie's face flushed and he closed his eyes.

Will turned to Shannon. "Take care of Rob, Shan. He has a liking for the things that interest me."

"I take care of them all, Will. You know that."

His eyes smiled at her, but he spoke to Robbie. "This one is a little different. I'll see you when you are out and about again. I can talk butterflies if you want to, but trees are more interesting."

"Trees are okay, too."

Shannon followed Will through the outer room and onto the porch. "Will?"

He turned to face her. "Are you keeping him here tonight?"

"I don't know. Should I?"

"It might be better for him if you did. He'll sleep better." He smiled at her again. "I'll be back. I have to write up a report for Miss Lucey and make sure everyone else is all right. A couple of the other boys looked a little ill. They were all kind of rattled."

"I'll probably be here. I'll stay here tonight if Robbie does."

She watched him until he was out of sight then went back to Robbie. He was lying on his back with his eyes closed, his hands crossed across his chest, fragile and vulnerable. She turned away, not wanting to disturb him if he had gone to sleep.

"Miss Conley?" Robbie said.

She turned toward him but he had not moved. "Yes?"

"Do I have to stay in bed?"

"The doctor said you should take it easy the rest of the day and stay off your foot."

He didn't move. She could see his disappointment.

Shannon sat beside him again wondering what he and Will had done together to form the obvious bond they shared, but it was absurd that she should want information about Will from this boy she didn't know.

He opened his eyes and stared at the ceiling.

For want of something better, she said, "You seem to get along quite well with Mr. Bonneville."

"He knows an awful lot about trees and plants and things." Robbie almost smiled. "The kind of stuff I like."

"He's a forester. He used to work for the state, and before that for a big lumber company. He knows a great deal about trees and I guess all of the other growing things out there in the forest."

"Then how come he's working here when he doesn't like it much?"

"How do you know he doesn't like it here?"

"He told me."

Surprised that Will had made such an admission to this boy, she asked, "Did you know Will . . . Mr. Bonneville, before you came here, Robbie?"

"No." He hesitated a long minute. "Do you know him real well, Miss Conley?"

"I've known him for several years."

"He said, just now, that I was different. What did he mean, just that I got hurt?"

The seriousness of his face disturbed her. "If Will said it, he meant it. What did you do to make yourself special?"

"I don't know. I've bothered him a lot." He turned toward her, his eyes big and sad. "He thinks I can't stand up for myself, that I can't do anything right. I don't know how to swim and I can't play baseball." He closed his eyes again. "That's what my father says, too. I'm chicken, and spineless, and, and I like girl things, like butterflies."

"Did Mr. Bonneville say that, Robbie?"

"No."

"He said you had the right answers. You must have done something right."

"I named some trees for him. Some the other guys didn't know."

"That would be enough to make you special as far as he is concerned, Robbie. Not many Rocky Point campers care enough to learn what he has to teach them."

"He was teaching me the names of the butterflies. I like to watch them and he loaned me a guide book so I could read about them. I didn't know there were so many kinds."

She wondered what it was that Will had found in this sad boy that had brought out his gentler nature, the side he kept hidden. "He doesn't often lend his books."

"No one ever loaned me one before."

"You've been to camp before?"

"This is the third time."

"Why do you keep going if you don't like it?"

Robbie closed his eyes again. "My folks take their vacation."

Was that what had roused Will's sympathy? She knew Will could find out a lot through casual conversation, a question here, a comment there, but she didn't know why he had bothered, why Will had taken so much time with a boy he had never seen before and would probably never see again. *Was Robbie what has been upsetting him so much lately?*

"He said he wanted to go back to his cabin," Shannon told Will later that evening as they sat on her cabin steps with iced tea. "Why did you think he should stay in the infirmary?"

Will didn't answer immediately. They were enjoying the peace and quiet of the thickening dusk, the coolness of the light breeze, the red dog sprawled at Will's feet. "Rob has a problem with his cabin-mates. A night away would have given him a break."

"He doesn't get along with them? A quiet boy like that?"

"That's the problem. He's a gentle sort." Will turned his head toward her but she couldn't really see his face. "They don't get along with him. He's different."

He took her hand and held it in both of his. "When I got married, I thought about the children we would have. My son would probably have been a lot like Rob."

"Why?"

"I was the different one when I was his age, the one who didn't play ball, who would rather read, the one who liked butterflies, except I liked birds. I could identify dozens of them by their calls."

"But you must have had someone who understood."

"My parents did. Rob's don't, apparently. At least, he doesn't think they do. I know that mine did and that made a lot of difference. Nobody seemed to think I was strange."

"Robbie told you all that?"

"He told me a lot more than he thinks he did."

She wondered aloud why he had asked the right questions.

He didn't answer for a long moment, then said bleakly, "He looks like Carol."

She couldn't answer because of a sudden sick feeling in the pit of her stomach and a suffocating tightness in her chest.

He squeezed her fingers. "Don't think that, Shan. I know he's given me a couple of sleepless nights, and he's made me think about things I didn't want to think about, but that's all."

She couldn't find an answer to that, either.

"Besides, thinking of Carol has made me realize how much you mean to me."

She glanced toward him, but he was watching Mick. "Are you sure, Will?"

"I loved Carol. She was beautiful, and I had never known anyone like her. I had never been in love before." He reached down and patted the dog. "I know now that she never loved me. She used me. That's the difference." He rubbed Mick's upraised head. "All I've had is Mick for a long time."

The dog was barely visible in the light spilling through the open door behind them. *I'm like Mick*, she thought, *silently devoted. Just hoping and waiting to be noticed.*

"I thought she had killed something in me and I didn't think I could ever love anyone again."

"I've loved you a long time, Will."

He turned toward her for a moment and then back toward the dog again. "I know that. And I'm grateful."

She couldn't answer that. What more could she say?

He sat still another long minute gently petting the dog. "Rob made me remember," he said finally. "She said she never wanted children. She asked me to have a vasectomy."

"And did you?" She tried to keep the question casual.

"No. I couldn't." He added after another long pause. "Rob looks enough like her to make me remember."

"Is he Carol's?" she asked, not really wanting to know the answer.

Will straightened, glanced at her, then stared out into the darkness for a long moment. "I don't know. The possibility is so remote I didn't even consider it. It is just a resemblance, a coincidence."

"And that resemblance makes you like him as you do?"

He leaned back, his elbows on the step. "It's more than that, I think. Rob pays attention to my talks. He likes trees. There are so few who do. Makes me feel like I'm accomplishing something."

"I understand." Will would naturally respond to interest. "And he likes you, too."

"Unfortunately." He got up slowly, carefully, and the dog got up, too, wagging his tail in anticipation of a walk. Will offered his hand to Shannon. "It's a nice night, after a long and not very good day. Shall we go up on top of the hill and watch the moon rise over the lake?"

11. ROBBIE

Robert Sullivan sat on his bunk with a notepad and pen and explicit orders from Mr. Perry to write a letter home. Everyone, they were told, had to have a letter ready to mail or no free time before supper. Robbie didn't think the directive was fair. He didn't want to write a letter, but he had no choice since he knew his mother expected one. His cabinmates were ignoring him, all busily scribbling, wanting to be done and outside playing again. Robbie didn't want to write, but he had nothing else to do, either, since he had no interest in the day's unscheduled time activities, baseball and free swimming. Mr. Bonneville was away somewhere doing something with another unit, even if Robbie had courage enough to look for him.

Robbie wrote carefully using his best handwriting, *Dear Mom and Dad,* and stopped. Could he write that he was having a great time when he wasn't? Of course, there was Mr. Bonneville and his nature walks, and he had managed to swim across the beginner's pool all by himself three times. He raised his head and saw Corey looking his way, but not really at him but apparently considering what to write. And there were *them*, too, and they weren't making his stay here much fun. Being constantly on edge and alert for pranks was hard on his stomach. He couldn't write about knotted pajama strings and his new sneakers dropped in a mud puddle.

He continued writing. *This is a nice camp. I'm in a cabin with five other guys named Corey, Art, Bert, Joe and Sam. They all like to play baseball.* Did that sound like he was playing baseball with them, too? He hoped it did. *I am learning to swim. Miss Susan is a real neat teacher.*

He spread out the pictures he had taken on his bunk: his cabin, three of his cabin-mates, Mr. Bonneville, Miss Susan, several of scenery, and four butterflies. He hadn't finished the roll because of his fall and the hornet stings, all of which were now just an unpleasant memory.

The packets of developed pictures had been distributed with supper last night. He had opened his immediately, as had everyone else at his table, and shared them with those sitting at his table, none of them his unitmates—he always made sure of that. He was not too unhappy with what he had taken—they were all in focus and none had his thumb on the side as he sometimes did, and one of the two of Mr. Bonneville was really good, but the other was blurred a little. One of them must have moved. Miss Conley had walked by and admired it.

The lady in the swim suit is Miss Susan, my swimming instructor. She's real nice.

He stopped again, looking at the picture of the dark haired girl in a life guard's jacket with a whistle around her neck. She was smiling, but not at the camera.

I can swim across the beginner's pool, and Miss Susan says I am almost ready for the big area.

That didn't sound like much of an accomplishment, so he added, *Miss Susan says I am non-buoyant and am doing real well and can learn to be a real swimmer.*

He looked at the pictures of Mr. Bonneville and remembered the horrible day when he had taken it. I *had a small accident the other day. I slipped and fell down a bank and landed in a hornets' nest and got stung seventeen times, but I'm all right now. I have a real nice nature counselor. His name is Mr. Bonneville, and he got me out of the hornets. He knows an awful lot and is teaching me all kinds of things about butterflies and trees and stuff.*

He decided to keep the best picture for himself. There probably wouldn't be another chance to take as good a picture.

He wished for a moment he had one of Miss Conley. *Our nurse is Miss Conley. She took me to the emergency room for my hornet stings, but the doctor said I would be all right and gave me a shot just in case because I had so many stings.*

He stopped again and thought about Miss Conley and Mr. Bonneville as he had heard them from his cot in the infirmary. They had sounded like his parents did sometimes when they didn't know he was listening. There was a softness in their voices that wasn't there when they were talking to him.

The thought struck him that they were in love, but that was absurd. Mr. Bonneville was so old. Robbie thought about that for a moment. Maybe Mr. Bonneville wasn't that old, even if his hair was sort of gray. *His hair is like mine,* he thought, *sort of darkish blond with streaks in it. Mine has yellow streaks and his has gray. Maybe the gray used to be blond.* The thought was a little comforting. And maybe Miss Conley was older than she looked. He knew some friends of his mother's like that.

And they called each other by their first names, Will and Shannon, he remembered. And they used the same tone his parents did when they said Morey and Carol. Except when his mother was mad, of course, or his father had had an extra drink or two. He didn't want to think about those times, so he re-read what he had written then added:

Miss Conley is real pretty, and real nice, too. She doesn't wear real nurse uniforms, just some pretty blue jackets. I think maybe I'll take a first-aid class that she teaches. Mr. Bonneville said we should all know first aid.

The letter wasn't as long as he knew his mother expected, so he added, *I'm sorry I didn't write before, but I've been awful busy. They don't give you much free time, and I've been spending most of my rest hours with Mr. Bonneville learning about butterflies and lichens and stuff.* He wished he had actually spent most of his free time with the counselor instead of just twice. *I really like our nature hikes. I signed up for as many as I could.* But he knew that nature walks were not why he had been sent to camp, so he continued, *There is a baseball game every afternoon between swimming lessons and supper. Some of the guys play tennis and badminton. There's an archery class I think I might get into, too.* He knew that committed him to at least one session, but he could stand a couple. He had tried archery once at school and it had been kind of fun.

The other boys had finished their letters and gone out, leaving him alone, and the quiet was pleasant, making it easier to think and compose a letter that he hoped would please his parents. He reread what he had written and was not satisfied with it. He thought about the previous day. *Miss Nancy has a crafts class that's kind of fun. We made things out of birch bark yesterday, canoes and picture frames. Miss Nancy is kind of homely.* That didn't sound too nice, even if true, so he added, *But she's nice, too. Kind of funny and she makes neat stuff.*

The first dinner bell sounded so he hastily added his love and good wishes and signed his name. He gathered up the pictures and sealed everything into one of the pre-addressed envelopes his mother had given him. He realized then that he had put both of Mr. Bonneville's pictures in but he didn't dare open the envelope to take it out. He didn't want to waste the stamp his mother had put on the envelope. He would have to account for them all.

There was nothing he could do about it now. He could get the pictures back when he got home. And there were the negatives in the packet. He took the letter with him and went to dinner.

12. WILFRED

An early morning shower and threats of more after breakfast persuaded Will not to make the scheduled jaunt with one of the girls' units, so he spent the morning in Kaflick with them, showing slides of pond water and the tiny creatures that live in it and looking at some of them through a microscope, eliciting a series of "eeyew" and "yuck" and "I'll never wade there again."

He enjoyed talking with the girls, liked their contagious laughter, their ability to see humor in almost everything, and their enthusiasms for whatever they were offered. They tended to be a little snide, of course, and catty, but they were much less physical than the boys and did not tire him. And they were, for the most part, pretty girls, all sizes, shapes and colors, but he still thought them pretty, and he had an enjoyable few hours, leaving him ready for whatever the rest of the day would bring. The sun came out bright and warm a little after ten o'clock, and by noon the grass was dry enough for comfortable walking. The air was still cool but washed clean of dust and pollen and breathing was easy.

He ate his lunch sandwiches in his own cabin, as he frequently did, sharing the cold cuts with Charlie the white cat and the crusts with Mick. When he left to return to the boys' unit, the dog followed him onto the porch, anticipating an invitation to go along.

"Sorry, Mick," Will told him. "As much as I'd like to take you, it's no dice. Miss Lucey doesn't even approve of you being here." He patted the dog. "So wait around a bit, old boy. I'll be back for you."

The setter lay down on the porch, resting his muzzle on his paws, and watched Will leave.

Will had no definite plans for his classes, leaving each day mainly up to the weather, his whim of the moment, and sometimes to what he discerned to be the mood of the campers . He considered several routes for the scheduled afternoon walk—he didn't consider what he did real hikes since he usually just strolled. He chose a longer route than his usual path, although it was a fairly easy one, and one they had not yet followed. He felt good, and was almost looking forward to it, in spite of knowing his lectures would mainly fall on deaf ears.

Unless, of course, it was Robbie's unit that was going. He checked the schedule and found it was. He recalled he hadn't taken this particular group out since Robbie's accident, nor had he seen Robbie. The boys had been involved for the past two days in arts and crafts, archery, and tennis. With Rob along, the outing might be worthwhile since the route was along the edge of the pond and up the brook with many natural wet areas to discuss. It was a trail he seldom took with a group of over-energetic boys because of the many temptations for horseplay. He saw Dan was again his assistant and decided to give him the role of disciplinarian. Dan liked keeping order.

He found his group more or less assembled when he arrived at the unit house. Dan had already checked footgear—socks and good sneakers were required—and the boys were ready to go. Robbie was standing alone as usual, not really part of the line, but he didn't speak to him. He did catch his glance before he addressed the group as a whole and silently acknowledged him. That was as far in that direction as he planned to go today.

"We're going to walking along the brook," Will told them. "The path is narrow in some places, and I don't want anyone falling in the brook, on purpose or otherwise. It's way too muddy. Mr. Dan is going to see to it that nobody does."

Dan grinned malevolently at them, and Will said, "All right, let's go."

Will walked slowly at the head of the line. He knew his leisurely pace sometimes irritated the boys who would have preferred to run, but there were a lot of things along this path for him to talk about: water plants such as pickerel weeds and arrowheads, cat tails, bur reeds, and button bushes, as well as a muskrat lodge, a log slide used by beavers, the shadowy haunts of the pickerel and horned pout, which he refused to call catfish in spite of that being their family even if he had to point that out. There were other types of aquatic wildlife, frogs and turtles and, if they were lucky, the great blue heron which occasionally fed along the shore. Much of what he said would go unheeded, but today he didn't mind. It was a lovely afternoon, just right for a stroll. *And how many things can go wrong on a leisurely nature hike?*

Will called a halt at the mouth of the brook, a gravelly delta where the small stream emptied into Pleasant Pond. The pond sparkled where the sun touched the tops of the ripples. There was just enough breeze to discourage insects, for which he was thankful since the damp areas tended to harbor mosquitoes. He had come this far without a twinge, and he still felt good. He knew that one person, at least, had listened to what he said, and today that one was enough. He sat down on a large stone.

But he wished Mick was with him. Or Robbie. He glanced around to see where the boy was, and saw him sitting on a log beside the path a little apart from the others. The other boys had divided themselves into noisy groups, most of them walking along the water and throwing stones. Dan sat beyond them, watching.

Remembering his own young days, Will asked, "Mr. Dan, do you know how to skip stones?"

"Sure." Dan stood up and selected a handful of small flat stones from the gravel. "Watch this." He stood sideways to the water, bent his knees slightly and sent a stone skipping across the water, bouncing in decreasing arcs until it sank.

"Four hops," Will said. "Not bad."

The boys surrounded Dan, clamoring for him to show them how to do it. Most of them failed, the stones simply sinking in the water, causing much laughter. An occasional success prompted more rivalry, more laughter, more horseplay.

Will saw that Robbie hadn't moved to join the rock skippers and broke one of his own rules. He said, "Rob, come here."

The boy looked up, surprise plain on his face, then rose slowly and came toward him. Will noted that several of the other boys interrupted their chatter for a moment and watched as Robbie stopped beside him.

"Sit down," Will said.

Robbie sat on the ground.

"You don't like to skip stones?"

"I tried it once and didn't do it very well."

"There's a knack to it." He again noted the interest of several of the others in what he and Robbie were doing. *Two of those are his bunkmates.* He returned his attention to the boy beside him. "In your studying, have you done much with wetlands?"

"No, sir."

"This is all new to you?"

"Most of it. I've read some."

"Have you been listening for the past half hour?"

"Yes, sir."

Will noted several heads together, Robbie's bunk-mates whispering while Robbie was staring silently at his feet. He regretted having spoken to the boy, showing his interest publicly. He knew too well what the other boys might have in mind. Favoritism was to be avoided. Will knew that.

Wilfred considered the path ahead and thought he knew where a plot could unfold. But there really was no way he could warn Robbie. It was one of those things that he had to cope with by himself. *And he has to learn to cope.* Surprised at the thought, he got up a little reluctantly and regarded the group for a moment before he said, "Okay, guys, that's enough rock skipping. Give it a try back at camp."

The boys formed their noisy line again. The path followed the bank of the brook, and here it was a good dry trail, a foot or more above water level, winding among the trees and ledges through which the brook flowed swift and clear. Will stopped frequently, pointing out deer tracks in the soft dirt, the scat of a muskrat, the marks of a beaver on a poplar tree, some differences in wet and dry land plants. He was being deliberately slower than usual.

They walked in single file on the narrow path. Will glanced along the line. The boy directly behind him was named Jeff, a nice, average, no-trouble-causing boy, one of the oldest in the unit. Robbie was behind him, too far away for Will to help, should the need arise. He fervently hoped it wouldn't. Robbie's cabinmates were toward the back, and there should be no problem.

The trail dipped into a swampy place. The brook widened into a sluggish stream, and the path was barely above the black oozy mud that bordered both sides. Reeds and an occasional clump of alders grew along the edge. There was water in dull pools beside the path, but at this time of year it was mostly black mud, at least ankle deep, thick and sticky.

Will stopped and looked back at the boys straggling along behind him. "Watch it," he said. "The path may be slippery."

He noted that the order of walkers in the line had changed. Jeff was still directly behind him, and then Robbie, but the next in line was Sam, followed by Corey and then Bert and Art. Corey was whispering to Sam.

Will stared at Robbie until the boy looked up at him. He shifted his glance to Sam and Corey still whispering, and Robbie turned his head to also look that way. Will turned away. Robbie had been warned and there was nothing else Will could do.

He walked slowly, describing the swamp growth but listening to the boys behind him. When he heard what he had been listening for, he turned around, almost colliding with Jeff. The plot unfolded as he had thought, but not as they had planned. Corey gave Sam a shove that should have made him stumble into Robbie, but Robbie had been forewarned, he was quick on his feet, and used to avoiding trouble. Robbie did not lose his balance completely, but caught one arm around a low hanging alder and only one of his feet went into the water. Sam, however, went face first into the slimy mud. Corey also caught his balance on a branch and avoided a fall.

Will pulled Jeff past him. "Go on up the trail a bit where it's higher and wait." He caught Robbie's free arm and jerked him back onto the path without looking at him. He was still watching the other boys behind him. Corey was laughing and helping Sam get out of the mud.

"Go up ahead with Jeff and stay out of trouble," he told Robbie, knowing that it was unjust and that he had said it too harshly.

Dan was shouting from the back of the line demanding order, but there was too much good-natured scuffling among the other boys, and Will knew what would happen next. He couldn't stop it, and it really didn't matter as long as no one got hurt. Long before Dan had restored order among the laughing and hooting boys, three more of them were in the mud, including Art and Bert. Of Robbie's cabin-mates, only Corey remained clean and the smug look on his face gave Will a slight chill.

But, again, there was nothing he could do. He said a little coldly, "Come on, cut out the foolishness. That mud doesn't really wash out, you know."

He kept Jeff and Robbie in front of him and led the boys out of the swampy place to where the brook again ran clear.

He stopped and told them to wash as best they could. He didn't look at Robbie, but he could see him trying to scrub the black ooze off his sneaker. Nor did he speak to the muddy boys. They were thoroughly enjoying themselves, and he did not interrupt their amusement. He recalled similar episodes from his own youth and kept his thoughts to himself. *Boys will be boys, and they always have been. But what does it bode for Rob since this time they failed? What else will they try since they are getting away with it this time?*

Will d stood aloof from them all, watching and waiting until Dan had finally had enough and yelled at them to shape up and ship out. They formed a straggling, laughing line which Will joined, but did not attempt to lead. The path was up hill from this point, and he was willing to simply walk along with them and forego his usual lectures. The path came out into an open field, bright with sunshine on tall grass, field daisies, tall buttercups, musk mallows and orange hawk weeds. At the top of the open space, they looked down on the lake and Camp Rocky Point. The path became a rutted road once used by the former farm and Will said, "All right, guys, there's the camp. Run if you want to."

Most of them took off in a whooping, shouting mass. Will stopped to watch them go. Dan and Robbie stopped beside him. "Don't you like to run, Rob?"

"Sometimes." The boy stared after the others but made no move to join them.

"Go on, run if you want to."

Robbie shook his head. "My sneaker's all wet. It squishes."

"Come along then," Will said, and started toward the camp at his own leisurely pace. Robbie followed, but said nothing.

"Mr. Bonneville, are you two related?" Dan asked from behind them.

Will looked back at him, then down at Rob's startled face. "Not that I know of. Why?"

"You two look alike. Not your faces," he added, "except your hair. I mean, you walk alike. From the back here, you look just alike."

Will smiled. "I don't think so, Dan. Do you, Rob?"

Robbie shook his head.

Will was a little bemused by the expression on Robbie's face, but he couldn't decide just what emotion had caused it. It was certainly surprise, but it was not one of dislike.

Dan laughed. "I meant it as a simple question. It just sort of surprised me." He paused. "Maybe it's because you don't usually single out one of the kids. I thought maybe he was a nephew or something."

Robbie said softly, "I wish I was."

Will half smiled. "Thanks, Rob." He gave him a small push down the path. "Run along now and catch up with the others. You'll miss your next class."

"I'd better catch up, too," Dan said, "and see what they're up and get them cleaned up. See you next hike."

"Sure thing, Dan." .

Will stood on the last rise above the camp. There was no one in sight, and he didn't continue down the hill, having no class scheduled and no other reason to go to his office. He cut across the face of the hill to his own cabin and sat on his own steps with Mick. He had much to think about.

Later that evening, sitting with Shannon in the pale moonlight on her cabin steps, he told her the long tale of wet and muddy campers, trying to make it a lot funnier than it actually was, and Miss Lucey's disgust at the dirty clothes, the sticky ooze staining the neat white camp shirts that would not wash out.

"But don't all boys act like that?" she asked. "They love mud and getting dirty."

"Yes, but this was deliberate. They intended to hurt or at least humiliate Robbie. They didn't plan to fall in, too."

She closed her fingers around his for a moment. "They didn't do it, so why worry about it?"

He turned his head enough to see her face. "I don't know, except that Robbie doesn't seem to have any defense against that sort of thing."

"There is no other reason?"

He considered the question carefully because he had wondered about it himself. "No other reason." He almost believed it.

She rested her elbow on the step behind her, her other hand still on his, and looked up at the darkening sky and the bright evening star just above the western horizon. "I'm sorry, Will. I didn't mean to say that."

He didn't answer for a moment, picked up her hand and held it between both of his, not looking at her. "It is exactly what you meant to say, Shan. You are thinking again about Carol, and the fact that I said Rob looks like her. Don't think that. Please don't."

"I'm trying not to, but, that boy . . . Robbie . . . keeps upsetting you, and I hate to see you upset."

"I probably needed to be upset, and don't take it out on Rob. It isn't his fault I like him. He listens to me." He drew her toward him and encircled her with his arm.

She pressed her face against his chest. "Will, I'm sorry. I'm just being silly."

"No, just normally curious." He paused a moment but she didn't speak. "Carol is gone, past, forgotten, and I am here with you."

"I know that, it's just . . ."

"You don't like to think about me having a wife somewhere."

"Have a wife?"

He heard the dismay in her voice. "*Had*, Shan. We were officially and properly divorced. And I don't think I ever really had her. Not her heart."

She didn't answer.

He released a long breath. "So, forget her, as I did,

as I want to again. And thinking about her isn't upsetting me, either. That is all over and done with." He paused, wondering again if that was really true, before going on. "Rob is nothing to me but a boy interested in butterflies, who happens to look a little bit like her."

Only he remembered what Dan had said this afternoon. *He looks like you.* "Who do you think he looks like, Shan?"

"Robbie? He doesn't look like anybody I ever saw. Only his hair, maybe. It has sun streaks in it like yours. What did yours look like before it turned gray? Were you blond like that?" She pushed herself upright and stared up at him. "Will . . .?"

He shook his head, smiling ruefully at her. "I have no children, remember? She didn't want any."

Shannon still looked doubtful, so he pulled her close again. She rested her head against his shoulder. "What made you ask that, Will?"

"It was something Dan said today, while we were hiking. He said we walked alike and wondered if we were related."

He felt her stiffen in his arms and held her away from him so he could read her expression. "Look, Shan," he said. "This is all foolishness. Robbie has nothing to do with me."

"But he upsets you. Every time you talk to him you get upset."

"No, not upset. He just makes me remember things I tried to forget. Now that I've thought about them again, and talked about them, I feel better about them. Maybe now I can forget them."

She met his eyes for a long moment. "Will, whenever you talk about her, it hurts you. I hate to see you hurt."

"Hurt?" he asked as he finally and deliberately recalled what he had so fervently tried to block from his memory. He closed his fingers tight around her upper arms and said with icy calm, "The last time I saw Carol she was in bed with . . . with . . ." The remembered name hit him solidly in the pit of his stomach, and he finished in a harsh whisper, "Morey Sullivan."

She opened her mouth to speak, but said nothing. Even in the shadows he could see the pain on her face and knew it mirrored his own, but he went on deliberately shocking her, and himself. "I had been away for a few days and came home earlier than I had planned . Apparently he moved in whenever I was gone."

"Oh, Will," she whispered.

"And I was gone quite a bit." The moonlight was pale on her face but he could see her concern for him. He hoped then that the telling of his story would finally free him from the nightmare that had been haunting him for the past twelve years. Shannon's face reflected everything Carol was not: kind, good, compassionate, and her love was given freely, willingly, with no thought of return.

With the full flood of relief that suddenly flooded him, he released her arms, held her close against him and buried his face in her hair. "Shannon, I love you."

"Oh, Will," she whispered against his chest, "I'm so sorry."

"It was a long time ago. I haven't seen her since. Not even at the divorce hearing. I let my lawyer take care of everything since she wasn't contesting anything."

He could feel Shannon crying against his chest and knew her tears were for him, but felt he did not deserve them. "It's all over," he said.

"Do you want to forget, Will?"

"I couldn't anyway, but it doesn't matter now. Shannon, you are so much more than she was. You know that I'll never see her again, and in another week or so I'll never see Robbie again." He paused then added, "You should be grateful to him for making me remember, making me think about all of this, and" —he held her even closer—"for making me appreciate you."

"Did he do all that? In two years I haven't meant anything to you?"

That hurt a little more than he cared to show. "You know you did. I have always cared. You have meant a great deal to me."

"Until a few days ago I only hoped. You never spoke to me of love, or much of anything else." She pushed herself way from him. "How many times have I told you I love you?"

"Too many times. And I never meant to tell you I've loved you for a long time. I didn't want you to know. I didn't want to hurt you. I love you too much to hurt you." He pulled her close again. "I don't want to spend the rest of my life hurting you. Shan, go away before it's too late."

"It was too late the first time I saw you. You needed me then, and now I need you."

"I still need you." He sat up straighter and moved a little away from her. "And I wish I didn't." He added, not meeting her eyes. "There is still my heart."

"I'd mend it for you if I could," she said.

"You have done your best. What more can you do?"

She leaned her head against him and he closed his arms around her. What else could he do but sit here and hold her and remember what he had tried so long to forget?

13. ROBBIE

Robbie Sullivan sat on the steps of his cabin after lunch, thankful that he could be alone for awhile. He had managed to escape the free swim time that his cabin-mates enjoyed. He didn't seem to be missed, but he stayed in plain sight in case a counselor was looking for him. He thought about getting Mr. Bonneville's butterfly book and reading about the skippers, but decided not to, even though he thought he had seen one earlier in the day.

Mr. Bonneville had told him to stay out of trouble, and he was determined to do that, even if the trouble was a kind not of his making. He recalled yesterday's walk along the brook and his near disaster in the swamp, and how only Mr. Bonneville's silent warning had saved him from falling in. He would be eternally grateful for that warning and he exulted a little. *They can't laugh at me over that! They are the ones who fell in. But what will they do to me because I didn't fall in? They planned that, so what are they planning now?*

But mostly he thought about what Mr. Dan had said, that he looked like Mr. Bonneville. He had thought about it a lot since yesterday afternoon. It was a nice idea, a wonderful idea, but he could not find any reason to think it might be true. Nowhere among his parents' relatives had he ever heard of a Bonneville. His mother was an only child, and his father's relatives all lived a long way away and most of them he'd never met. He had met his two half-siblings and their parents a couple of times but knew nothing about their mother, nor his father's previous marriage. He didn't know why, but it was something no one mentioned and he had no reason to ask.

Robbie indulged in a pleasant day dream, an escape he rarely allowed himself because of the longing he could build up and the hurt which inevitably followed when the dream was destroyed. But he let himself think about it now. If Mr. Bonneville really was an uncle, or a cousin maybe, one everyone had forgotten about, maybe they would let him spend his three weeks with him instead of at some dumb camp.

His practical mind gave him another answer. *Just come back to Camp Rocky Point next summer. Mr. Bonneville lives here, and he'll be here again next year.* But it would be so much nicer if he was an uncle. *Maybe I could live up there in his cabin and not have to stay down here, and only go to the classes I like.* He looked toward the lake, still enjoying the idea, and watching two canoes coming across the lake toward him.

He didn't like to watch boats on the lake. He had never been in a canoe or even a rowboat, and this camp forbade non-swimmers their use. His previous camp did not have a waterfront, just a swimming pool. He looked down at his feet again and thought about his nature teacher, recalling the moment that Mr. Bonneville had spoken to him, called him to him, how good it had felt to be singled out for once, noticed by someone he admired. And Mr. Bonneville liked him. He knew it, he could feel it in his heart, and it was a warm feeling he could keep and hold to himself to remember later.

Here was someone he liked and admired, who liked the things that he, Robbie Sullivan, liked, who didn't make fun of him for liking butterflies, who understood about his not liking baseball, who knew why he couldn't swim very well. And in another week Robbie would be leaving, going back home.

But, Robbie thought, some hope returning, *maybe I could write to him. I can ask him if I can write to him.* Preoccupied as he was with that cheering thought, he didn't notice his cabin-mates until they were all around him. With cold fear tightening his chest and settling in his stomach he tried to get up, escape whatever they had in mind for him, knowing that it would not be pleasant, that he could be in trouble again, in spite of his efforts. "What do you want? Let me alone."

Corey laughed at him, a harsh rasping sound that left Robbie chilled. "You're coming with us, Robbie."

"No. I don't want to go anywhere."

"But you are," Sam said. "Now."

Robbie resisted, pulled back against their hands, dug in his elbows, but they caught his arms, pulled him off the step and onto his feet. Bert and Art were both bigger than Robbie, and Corey walked behind, pushing him a little. They quickly rounded the cabin to be out of sight of the unit house and started up the path to the top of the hill.

Alarmed, Robbie demanded, "Where are we going? What are we going to do?" He looked around for help but saw none.

Corey laughed again, a deep, dark kind of laugh. "You'll see."

They propelled him around to the back of the row of cabins, off the graveled path and angled across the face of the hill toward the old barn, to where Robbie knew they were not supposed to go. He protested their route. "We're not supposed to go there. You know that."

"Don't worry, Robbie," Corey said. "Nobody's going to see us go. Mr. Perry's too busy with the archery class to notice that we aren't there. Bert told him we were going to a craft class."

"Yeah," Art said, "and Mr. Bonneville's over at Kaflick in his office."

"He's not going to rescue you this time, Robbie."

Robbie looked up the hill at the barn that had been emphatically declared off-limits to all campers. A cold hard lump settled in his stomach . He couldn't say anything and he could barely breathe.

"We going inside this time, Corey?" Bert asked.

"No, around back's all right. We just need to be out of sight."

Robbie found strength enough to resist again, stiffening his legs and dragging back on the arms that held him. He didn't say anything, reserving what strength he had to fight with. He knew his predicament was hopeless, that there was no one to rescue him, but he tried, struggling against them until they rounded the end of the barn. The grass on this side had not been mowed, and it was over knee high, dry and patchy with weeds. A few broken boards had been piled against the side of the barn, and it was on these that Art and Bert pushed Robbie down and sat beside him to hold him there.

Corey stood in front of him, laughing down at him. "We think it's time you grew up, Robbie. We don't like mama's boys who go running and crying to counselors every time they stub their toes."

"Or who run around chasing butterflies," Bert said, laughing. "No way for a real guy to act. Butterflies are for sissies."

"Or who thinks he knows more than we do," Art said. "I don't like that. You're a show-off. How come you know all those tree names anyhow?"

Robbie didn't answer. Being a Boy Scout would not be high on their list and would add to their teasing. He could think of nothing to say, no way to defend himself. He fought down the familiar sickness beginning in his stomach, and glared back at Corey as steadily as he could. "I just like those things. And it's none of your business. What I do."

"We think it is." Corey pulled an open pack of cigarettes from his pocket and held them out toward Robbie. "First, a cig."

Robbie said fairly steadily and fighting the rising bile in his throat, "I don't smoke."

Corey laughed. "Then it's time you learned, old as you are."

"Thanks, no."

Art laughed. The others took cigarettes and lit them with a match book, and one was forced between Robbie's clenched lips. Corey laughed as he held the cigarette in Robbie's mouth.

Robbie tried to spit out the cigarette but Corey was stronger and he had no choice but to draw in the mouthful of smoke. He coughed, choked, losing the cigarette, and they released him, laughing.

"Now that wasn't too bad, was it, Robbie? Maybe you'll grow up yet." Corey picked up the cigarette again.

Robbie scowled at Corey's smirking face, but when he opened his mouth to answer, the cigarette was shoved in again hurting the side of his mouth.

"You're doing fine," Corey told him.

Bert and Art held Robbie's arms and kept him sitting on the pile of boards, while Corey held the cigarette in his mouth, forcing him to breathe through it. He coughed again, and knew he would be sick to his stomach. *Serve them right*, he thought, *if I throw up all over them.* He gagged, choked, and Corey laughed, a mocking kind of laugh that made Robbie mad enough to let him gain some control of his stomach. His anger gave him some courage and he blew hard. The cigarette landed in the grass at his feet.

Bert reached for the still smoking cigarette but a booted foot stepped on it first. Robbie looked up at Mr. Bonneville and was almost sick to his stomach again.

The counselor was scowling at them, his anger obvious. "All right," he said. There was a chill in his voice that made Robbie wince. "Pick it up and get down to Miss Lucey's office. Now!"

The others got up slowly, muttering, but not really saying anything. Robbie didn't move; he didn't trust his legs to let him stand up or carry him steadily.

Mr. Bonneville snapped, "This way. Move!"

They went except for Robbie who still couldn't move his frozen limbs. Mr. Bonneville's hand closed tight around his upper arm and jerked him to his feet. "You, too. Come on."

Robbie stumbled a few steps beside him, fighting the sudden hot tears he didn't want to shed and shame himself further, trying to keep some shred of dignity and self-respect. The hand that had comforted him, encouraged him, was now hard, hurting his arm, and that sharp pain gave him a small measure of control over the rising sickness. When they were around the barn and in the road again, Mr. Bonneville released his arm and gave him a small push to keep him walking in front of him with the other boys.

Robbie did as he was told, marching in line behind Sam while concentrating on keeping his unruly stomach under control. Afraid that he was losing the battle, he said, "I'm going to be sick."

Mr. Bonneville said coldly, harshly, "No, you aren't. You've used that excuse too many times. You don't have to be sick if you don't want to be."

Robbie kept his mouth shut and swallowed the bitter bile.

He waited on the porch in front of Miss Lucey's office with the others while Mr. Bonneville explained to her what had happened, how he had found the boys behind the barn, what they were doing.

Miss Lucey called to them, told them to come in, and Mr. Bonneville came out, still scowling, not looking at them.

Robbie touched his arm timidly as he went by. Mr. Bonneville looked down at him without speaking. Robbie said, scarcely more than a whisper, "I didn't want to go up there. They made me."

"Nobody can make you do anything you don't want to do."

Robbie turned away and went into Miss Lucey's office, fighting tears and trying to keep at least some of control of himself. His hoped for world was gone, turned upside down. What was he to do now?

14. WILFRED

Wilfred Bonneville sat at the cluttered table in his cabin and ate a late supper of mac and cheese, depressed by the afternoon's events and annoyed with Robbie's cabinmates. He considered the boys as he had seen them when he had come around the corner of the barn, alerted to their presence by Corey's harsh laughter. He could see what they were doing, and it had made him angry, angry enough to take out his irritation on Robbie as well as the others. But perhaps his anger had kept Robbie from vomiting and losing what little dignity he had left. He was annoyed with Robbie as well, not for being what he was—there was little he could do about that—but for not trying to do anything about it, even to defend his right to be that way. It was distressing to see him so resigned to being pushed around by everyone when he could at least make an effort, take a stand, if he dared.

He poured himself a second cup of coffee and thought of Shannon instead, about the pleasure of being with her a little later in the evening when she was through with her duties. He wondered what he should, or could, say to her, how to explain a recent and unexpected turn of events in his life, possible changes that he had ignored until now. Until he had Shannon to consider.

A letter lay on the table in front of him. He had read it twice and set it aside to consider more carefully . Its contents represented a temptation almost as great as Shannon herself, and he didn't want to think about it just then, even though it offered him what he wanted most to do, to return at least partly to his former life, an escape from Camp Rocky Point.

Do I dare take the chance with my heart the way it is? Can I go back, do it by myself? Would Shannon go with me? Would it be fair to ask her? Ask her to share what time I have left? And how much time is that?

Beside him, Mick's tail thumped on the floor. The dog had lifted his head and was staring intently at the door. His tail thumped again.

"Shan already, Mick? It's too early for her."

The dog got up and went to the screen door. He stood there a moment, intent on something outside, then pushed the door open with his nose and went out, the screen door banging shut behind him. Will sat still waiting for Shannon's usual cheery greeting to the dog, but it was a boy's voice he heard, a soft voice saying, "Hello, Sir Richard."

Will recognized the voice, released a long shuddering breath, resigned himself to the inevitable painful confrontation, and got up. He opened the door and stepped onto the porch. Robbie was kneeling in front of the dog, both arms around his neck, and his face was buried in Mick's soft coat. Mick responded with a face lick, his tail wagging.

Will said as coldly as he could muster, "This place is off limits to campers, Robbie. You know that."

Robbie looked up at him but didn't let go of Mick. "Yes, sir, but I had to talk to you."

"Aren't you in enough trouble already?"

Robbie rubbed his face on Mick's head again and didn't answer.

Will wondered if the boy was crying and trying not to. He sat down on the top step. "Come here, Rob."

Robbie sat on the step below him, but kept his eyes on the dog which had followed him.

Will had control of his voice again. "All right, what did Miss Lucey say?"

"She told us how stupid we were, and how bad smoking is for our health, and how we weren't supposed to be up by the old barn, and how we could have set a fire in the dry grass." His voice trembled and he hesitated a moment. "I knew all that. I told them, my cabinmates, that."

"And what did she do about what you did?"

Robbie kept his eyes on the dog. "She said she wished that she could take a strap to us, but since she couldn't do that we are all on probation and can't take the trip in to town tomorrow that was planned, and if we get into any more trouble we'll be sent home."

"That would be one way to get out of here."

"I wouldn't go home. I don't think my parents are home from Bermuda yet. I'd have to go to my grandfather, and he'd take a belt to me, first thing. I don't think he likes me very much."

Will couldn't answer. Robbie's situation was too sad. "So why did you come up here if you are supposed to be staying out of trouble?"

"I asked Jeff to tell Mr. Perry I was talking to you. Nobody will come looking for me for a while."

"Why, Robbie?"

He glanced up at Will and then back at the dog. "Because I didn't go up to the barn on my own. They took me. They made me go."

"They couldn't have if you'd really wanted to stay put."

"How, Mr. Bonneville? They're bigger than me and stronger. They could hurt me. They did hurt me."

"Yes, but you have to make a choice sometimes. Do you believe enough in your own ideas to fight for them?"

"I can't fight." There was certainty and resignation in his voice, but Will understood.

"Maybe," Will said, "but how much resistance did you put up when they gave you the cigarette? You had it in your mouth."

"There were five of them and they were holding my arms."

"I know that, Rob. I'm not condemning you for being there. I'm saying that you let everyone else make your decisions for you. When are you going to stand up for what you think is right?"

He didn't answer for moment and continued softly stroking the dog. Then he said faintly, "But no one else thinks like I do."

"Does that make any difference?"

"It does to my parents."

Will thought about that for a moment and watched Robbie petting Mick, gently rubbing his ears. He had never seen Mick take to a child as he had to Rob and wondered why. "So why did you have to come up here and tell me this?"

"Because I think that maybe you think like I do. I want to learn about things you know." He turned enough so that he could look up at Will. "Nobody ever understood me before."

"Understood what?"

Robbie turned away again. "Like why I get sick to my stomach so easy. And why I can't swim. And why I'd rather read than play games. Except checkers."

"Did you ever play chess?"

"I had a teacher who taught me and played a few games, but then we moved. Now I just play checkers." He rubbed Mick's ears for a moment. "Dad won't play with me anymore because I always beat him."

"Take up tiddly winks," Will said.

Robbie turned around and glanced at him.

"You'd better get back to camp. It won't take Mr. Perry very long to figure out that I'm not at Kaflick and that you are missing again. Don't get in trouble twice in one day, especially if you don't want to be sent to your grandfather."

Robbie got up slowly.

"Keep in mind what I said, Rob. You don't have to do anything you don't really want to do. You might get in trouble by not doing it, and you might get hurt, but the choice is yours. Don't do things that are completely against your thinking simply because some bully says you have to. You're smart enough to know what's right for you and what isn't."

Robbie made no move to leave.

"Rob," Will said earnestly, "you are up here where you aren't supposed to be, and if you get caught, you know what will happen. And there is nothing I can do to save you."

Robbie turned away without speaking.

"I'll talk to you tomorrow."

Robbie glanced back at him. "Thank you, sir." He turned to run down the path and Will had to call to Mick to come back.

"What's the matter with you, old thing? What do you see in that boy?"

Mick wagged his tail, still looking down the path that Rob had taken. "No, you can't go. Wait a while and I'll take you for a walk."

But Mick didn't lie down and after a moment Shannon came up the path. Will met her at the bottom of the steps, hugged her and kissed her lightly on the cheek.

"Will, what was Robbie doing up here?"

"Visiting."

"Against the rules? He knows better than that."

Will sat down on the steps again and she sat beside him. "You must have heard all about his mis-adventures today, his cabin-mates latest."

"Of course, but—"

Will put his arm around her and said, "Mick likes him."

Shannon patted the dog. "Miss Lucey is very upset about it, Will."

"About their smoking? All kids try it."

"That, too, but mostly about their being up by the barn. They could have started a fire in the dry grass."

That was what bothered him, too. The unmown grass and weeds back there were very dry and it was out of sight of the camp. A fire could have gotten a good start before anyone noticed it, and the barn was all dry wood and would burn quickly, like tinder.

"And if she finds out he was up here—"

"I won't tell her. Come on, Shan, cheer up. I've had all the gloom and doom I can stand for one day."

She smiled up at him.

"And Mick wants to take a walk." He got up and offered her his hand. "And I need a nice change of scenery, some fresh air to clear my mind."

She didn't question his offer, rose and followed him.

He led her up the hill behind his cabin, away from the camp, along the path that he sometimes walked with his campers, until they came to a high meadow full of tall grass, field daisies, pink musk mallows, and giant mullein just coming into flower. He sat down on a wide ledge and held his hand out to her. "This is a good place from which to watch a sunset."

She settled herself beside him.

The lake far below them was growing dark in the shadows creeping across from the farther hills, lit only by the lambent light. The bright gold and orange striped sky made stark black silhouettes of the rounded hills.

"If it were always like this, I could stay here forever." He thought again of the letter lying on his table with his dirty supper dishes. "But it isn't."

"Where do you want to go, Will?"

He knew what he wanted, wanted desperately: to accept the offer in the letter from his former boss, to leave this camp he so heartily disliked. But he also knew, had forced himself to accept, that he could not go alone, and wondered if she would go with him. *Maybe I should take the advice I just gave Rob. I know what I want to do, that it's the right thing for me, but I don't know if it's right for her. Isn't that her decision to make? Am I trying to make her decisions for her?*

"I had an offer," he said tentatively. "A different job, a real one."

She turned to face him. "From who? To go where, do what?"

He took her hand in both of his, holding her beside him. . "I got a letter today from my old boss. He wrote to me once before, after I got out of the hospital, but then I didn't feel I could do the work, that I wasn't up to it. I didn't want any of them pitying me. I took a leave of absence. It's still in effect."

"Where, Will?"

He heard the tremor in her voice, her uncertainty. "I worked for the state Forest Service, you know that. Joe said my job is still there waiting for me. Someone has retired and his place could be mine. As it would have been before. . ." He didn't finish the thought.

"Could you do it? I mean . . ."

He didn't answer for a long minute, recalling the duties of the position, knew that he probably could, or adapt the responsibilities to what he could manage. It was a job that he could do mainly as he saw fit, that he could devise for himself within the parameters of the position.

"I'm sorry, Will, I didn't say that right."

"It was what you meant. Am I physically capable of going back to a real job?" He knew there was bitterness in his voice and was sorry for it. None of this was her fault. She had nothing to do with the heart attack that changed his life.

"I just don't want you killing yourself, and I know you aren't happy here." She paused, her face still toward the fading colors of the setting sun. "Are you still afraid of other people, what they will think?"

"I wasn't afraid of that before. Too proud, maybe, stubborn, but not afraid."

She looked down at her hand still held tightly in his. "It would be the right thing for you to do. I want you to be happy."

He knew then that she would not ask him to take her with him. She would let him go because it was what he should do. He would break her heart if he left her here, and he couldn't do that. He would be breaking his own.

"Shan," he said softly.

She watched him without speaking, and even in the growing darkness, he could see the love in her eyes, and the unshed tears. But he could not make himself say the words he wanted to say. "Shall we go back down before it gets too dark to see the trail?"

She nodded, and he got up, offered her his hand.

They strolled down the hill, his hand in hers, but neither of them spoke. At the bottom of the cabin steps he said, "Come in. Read the letter for yourself."

"All right."

She didn't comment on the uncleared table and the general clutter of the room as she sometimes did. She sat in one of the two chairs and took the letter he handed her.

He leaned against the sink on the other side of the small room, his arms crossed over his chest, watching her read. He studied the wave in her hair, the way it curled over her ear, observed her slim fingers holding the letter as she tipped it toward the light from the table lamp to see better. She wore no rings. He hadn't thought about that before, but knew she wore little jewelry other than a plain gold wrist watch and occasionally a gold chain with a rose pendant that had been her grandmother's.

Rings? It would be a way to ask her without really asking. And easier for her to say no. "Shan . . .?"

She looked up from the letter and met his gaze. "Yes?"

He could see her uncertainty. "Wait there a moment, will you?" He went into his back room, the room he used for sleeping and storing his few belongings. Where had he put it? He stood in the middle of the tiny room and looked at the narrow bunk, the scarred three-drawer chest beside it, the old chair piled with his extra clothes. He knelt and opened the bottom drawer of the chest and rummaged among the boxes and papers, but couldn't find what he sought.

From his position on the floor, he noticed the old foot locker under his bed and smiled, knowing that was where he had put it. He pulled it out and opened it. Beneath his winter coat was a shoe box-sized cedar jewelry chest , an old box deeply carved with twining leaves and dogwood flowers, secured with a small gold hasp and heart-shaped padlock. He got clumsily to his feet, found a key chain in a pottery dish on top of the dresser and returned to the outer room with the box in his hand.

Shannon was sitting in her chair, still holding the letter with both hands staring at it.

Will sat down beside her, pushed aside his supper dishes, and put the box on the table. He found a tiny gold key among the several on the chain and fitted it into the lock. She watched him but didn't comment.

"This box was one of my mother's favorites. It belonged to my grandmother. Ed has about everything else of hers."

The lock opened reluctantly—when had he last opened it? What reason had he had to even think about it?—but eventually he could remove the padlock and push back the cover to reveal the jumble of little boxes and pieces of jewelry it contained. He picked out a worn and faded blue velveteen ring box and opened it. Seeing the three oval opals set in old-fashioned gold filigree brought sudden fond memories of his mother, the tough but gentle woman who had worn this ring so often.

He took the ring out of the box. "Shan, your hands are small like hers were." It was not the way he wanted to say it. He wasn't saying anything right. Was he doing anything right? He picked up her left hand and put the ring on her third finger. "Unless you happen to be superstitious about opals, think they're bad luck or something if you aren't born in October. . ."

She gasped, closed her hand over the ring, holding it tight as if he might take it back. "Oh, Will."

He saw the tears on her cheeks, but there was nothing he could do but hold her tight. "I'd rather give you her diamonds," he said into her hair, "but Ed took them for his Nancy."

She pulled away from him so she could open her fingers and hold her hand so she could see the ring in the lamp light. "Will, this is beautiful, so very beautiful."

"Mother wouldn't give me anything for Carol, but I know she'd want you to have this."

"I'll be proud to wear it, Will."

He held her away from him, far enough so he so he could study her face. "When this camp season is over," he said. "Does that give you time enough?" He still couldn't say the right words. He couldn't remember how he had proposed the first time, but those words would not be right for Shannon.

"Will, I'd marry you tomorrow."

"I'll write to Joe, and tell him this fall, that I'm committed here until the middle of August anyway. Is that all right?"

"Anything you say is fine."

Will cupped his hands around her face and looked seriously at her. "I shouldn't do this to you, shouldn't ask you to come with me. It isn't fair to you, but I can't help it. I need you, Shan."

"I'd go anywhere with you, Will. I was so afraid when I read the letter that you would leave me here. That I was just part of this camp you want to leave."

"I can't go alone. I thought I was self-sufficient, but I'm not."

"I'm glad you aren't."

"And this isn't the way I intended to ask you. Nothing came out the way I planned it."

"I don't mind. Really I don't."

"I will have to leave so many things for you to do. It isn't fair to ask this of you."

"Will, don't. Don't spoil this for me."

He drew her against him again, his face in her hair. "You are the only good thing about this whole damn camp. If I live through this summer, I'll never set foot in another one."

"I hope we never have to."

"We," he said. "That sounds so much better than me."

She said, "It will always be we, us, the two of us together."

He fervently hoped so.

15. SHANNON

Shannon sat on the edge of her bed, not quite believing what had happened after so many months of forlorn hoping, that Will had actually asked her to marry him, in his roundabout way. She admired the three opals gleaming softly on her finger, moving her hand so they would catch the light. The ring was loose, not quite fitting, but she would not mention it to Will; a discreet piece of tape would solve the problem until she could have it resized. She had not yet totally accepted that he had actually given a ring to her, one that had been his mother's, and he had, in a round-about fashion, asked her to marry him. She had been living that dream for so long.

The letter with the job offer, giving him a chance to leave the camp and go back to his former beloved way of life, and to where she might never see him again had left a pain in her heart and a sickness in the pit of her stomach. But Will was so unhappy at Rocky Point, she wouldn't have said anything to prevent his going, no matter how much his leaving would hurt. She loved him too much to hold him back. And now she didn't have to think that way any longer. At the end of the summer, he'd said , after the camp closed.

Shannon closed her hand, still studying the slightly tarnished gold ring, and then opened her hand again to admire the effect. It was a beautiful piece in a nice old-fashioned way, so different from the modern stark settings she had seen in jewelry stores. Opals were really out of fashion these days. Diamonds and the more brilliant emeralds and rubies were much more popular.

Opals are like Will, she thought, not at all flashy, full of hidden fire. It just takes the right light to see it. I wonder what his mother was like. He said the ring was hers, the only thing of hers that he had, yet he gave it to me. That thought caused her to pause, consider the small thrill it brought her. *I wonder why he never talks about his family. But, I don't talk about mine, either. But what had he said about superstition, that opals were bad luck?*

She recalled having heard that somewhere, that no one but October-born people should wear opals. *My birthday is in May, but I don't need emeralds. What bad luck can such a lovely ring bring anyone? And it was his mother's. That has to count for something.*

She lay down, knowing sleep was a long way off. She had way too much to consider. In a half-dream state, she visualized the satin and lace wedding gown with a train and floor-length veil that she'd chosen, come close to buying, for her other planned wedding, the elaborate church ceremony with a dozen attendants, the grand event she had planned with her mother for her marriage to Jimmie. That sort of extravaganza was not for Will, nor for her any more. She knew their wedding had to be something simple, with just family and a few close friends. Tomorrow she would call her mother and her sister Fern.

Unless, of course, he has second thoughts.

She squelched that thought, along with a fleeting reminder that the stress of all of this could bring on another heart attack. She had a brief surge of panic but a few deep breaths relieved it: she had lived with that fear for too long for it to affect her now. *Will will be fine. This will relieve some of his fears, give him something to look forward to, a place other than this, his old job back, a definite release of stress.*

She knew she needed rest, but she wasn't yet ready to sleep. There was still too much to think about. She wondered where they would live, where in the state Will would work, what he would be doing, would there be a hospital near enough for her to work? She would have to work.

The letter hadn't said because Will's boss already knew where and how he was living when he had the heart attack. There was so much about Will that she didn't know: his past, his family, his work. But there was a lot about him she did know, all of the really important parts. His gentleness, his strength of purpose, his vast knowledge of the forests, his stubbornness when he knew he was right, his love of the wild, all of those things that endeared him to her.

And I love him so much!

She closed her eyes and let herself dream about his arms around her, holding her close as he had a little while ago when he had said good night. She could feel his comforting strength. *As soon as this camp session is over, it will be forever. And I won't miss working here, either. There are so many other places I can work.*

A thought of his precarious health, his weakened heart, again intruded, but she dismissed it. He might not, probably wouldn't, live a great many more years. But any time at all with him would be worth the heart ache afterward.

She wondered if they could have children. *He will be a wonderful father. Just think how he is with Robbie.*

She knew she was being idealistic, probably unreasonable, not considering some very real possibilities, but Will deserved a little happiness, too, after all that had been done to him, all Carol had done, all Robbie was doing. Will was so much more a man than Jimmy ever was, could ever be.

16. WILFRED

Will ate his cold lunch in his cabin with Mick and Charlie, again carefully considering what he planned to do during the campers' free time after lunch and the possible consequences of his actions. He decided the satisfaction he would get out of it offset any displeasure on the part of Amanda Lucey. He was tired of her rigid rules, petty tyrannies, and her apparent inability to listen to anyone else, or even to reason. *I won't be here much longer anyway. She'll have to find someone else to lord it over. I've made my decisions and can tell her what I think.*

Will found that thought satisfying enough to firm his resolve to make Robbie happy for at least one afternoon, to give him one thing he really wanted but couldn't have simply because of Miss Lucey's draconian rules. He knew there was no way he could be replaced this late in the camp season, he would not be dismissed whatever came of this, but that was not part of his present reasoning. He put his plate and glass in his tiny sink then selected two fishing poles and a tackle box from the collection stacked behind the bedroom door. He invited the dog to come with him and was at the boys' dock before he heard the campers returning from lunch for their rest period, rest few of them ever took. He put the fishing gear into a small rowboat tied to one side of the dock, went into the boathouse for a pair of oars and took two life jackets from their rack. He put the oars in the boat, dropped the vests on the plank walkway, told Mick to get into the boat and wait for him, and then walked up the rise into the boys' unit.

He met Perry outside his cabin. "I'm going fishing," he said. "Out in the lake."

Perry looked at him with mild surprise. "Why tell me?"

"I'm taking Robbie with me."

"Isn't he a non-swimmer?"

"He's learning."

"But, Miss Lucey ordered—"

"I have never agreed with that order. If she should find out, I'll take the blame for it. It won't be your problem. He'll be perfectly safe with me."

Perry shrugged and turned away. "What you do is up to you, Mr. Bonneville. Not my concern."

"Rob has a need. He's never been in a boat."

"I won't tell on you."

"I didn't think you would, but you happen to be his unit leader, and you are supposed to know where he is at all times."

Perry laughed. "Well, now I know where he'll be. Have fun." He glanced at the cabins behind him. "Rob is a sad little sort. This might do him some good."

"That is kind of what I thought."

Will crossed the path to the cabin Robbie shared with his bullying mates, pushed open the door and looked inside. Four of the boys were sitting on the floor playing cards and one was watching. Robbie was sprawled on his bunk with a book. They all turned toward him questioning.

"Rob, come out here," Will said.

The boy got up slowly, put his book on his bunk.

Will stepped out and waited.

Robbie came hesitantly, not speaking, looking at Will apprehensively, and closed the screen door behind him.

Will said, "Come on," and turned toward the dock, not waiting to see if Rob were behind him. He picked up a life jacket and handed it to the boy. "You do like fishing, don't you?"

"I guess so."

"You don't know?"

"I've only been a couple of times and never in a boat."

"Well, this time you're going." He picked up his own life jacket and shrugged into it. "Put it on, Rob, you have to wear it and we don't have much time for this expedition."

Robbie struggled into the jacket while following Will along the dock.

Will turned to Robbie. "Okay, get in, up front there with Mick." He watched the boy step cautiously over the side of the dock, placing his feet carefully, holding onto the side of the boat as it rocked. When Robbie was seated, he unfastened the mooring line, stepped in, settled himself on the seat, then pushed the boat away from the dock.

The day was warm, sunny with a light breeze. Fluffy cotton ball clouds edged the bright blue sky and were piling up along the western horizon. Rowing was easy and an activity Will enjoyed whenever he could. He worked at it leisurely, but he wanted to be out of sight of the camp as quickly as possible. He could hear Robbie talking softly to the dog, but he didn't listen to what the boy was saying. *Every boy should have a dog, at least some kind of pet. Or a brother.*

He wondered why he was doing this. His promise to talk with Robbie today had not included a forbidden boat trip. And he wondered, too, about his sudden perverse desire to provoke Amanda Lucey, and disregard those rules that he had long considered wrong.

He rounded the point and the camp was no longer visible. The narrow brook along which they had walked was ahead of them, and it was there, where the currents eddied, that he intended to fish for the lake trout that frequently gathered there. He shipped the oars, pulling them into the bottom of the boat, and turned toward Robbie.

"Here we are."

Robbie had one arm around the dog, the other trailing in the water. He turned shining eyes toward Wilfred, but didn't say anything.

Will picked up a fishing pole.

"Do I have to fish?" Robbie asked. "Can't I just sit here?"

Will shrugged and put the pole down again. "If that is what you want. I only came out here so we could talk without being disturbed and fishing is a good excuse. I did promise you we'd talk."

Robbie looked into the clear water and didn't answer.

Will could see that the boy was looking at a spot where the bottom pebbles were clearly visible, water weeds swayed gently with the current from the brook, and small fish moved in and out of weeds, a view Wilfred had always found mesmerizing. He shook off the feeling. That was not the reason he had come here. "You were anxious enough to talk to me last night. You broke the rules to do it."

"Isn't this breaking the rules, too?"

"It is, but I'll take responsibility for it. You should be perfectly safe out here with me."

"Is that what you meant about doing what I wanted to do?"

"In a way. I wouldn't advise you to just take one of the boats and go rowing off somewhere. The boats aren't yours, and you don't know how to handle them. This happens to be my boat, not the camp's. You do have to follow rules to get along in this world."

Robbie looked into the water again still trailing his fingers in the easy current.

"What I meant was standing up for what you think. If you like to chase butterflies, then I would go and chase butterflies, no matter what your cabin-mates think about it. They play ball without considering how you feel about it."

"Everybody plays ball."

"I don't. I never did unless it was required by my teacher for a class or something. I never played by choice."

Robbie's eyes were wide, but he said nothing.

"I managed to grow up without playing baseball. Or soccer or basketball. I did like ice skating."

Robbie still didn't comment.

"My brother liked all those things I didn't, but we still managed to get along all right together."

"I don't have any brothers. There's just me."

"That might make it harder right now, but you can still maintain your integrity."

"But my folks think I should be like everyone else."

"That does present a problem. You can't really go against their wishes entirely. Not yet anyway."

Robbie buried his face in Mick's thick red fur. "I can't even have a dog. No pets at all. I wanted a hamster once but my mother doesn't like them. She said she didn't like animals and we move too often."

Will had no answer for that. He didn't know what else to say about Rob's problems, either, or why he was even trying. "You just have to make the best of it."

"If they would only take me with them once when they go somewhere, instead of sending me to camp."

Will heard that as a plea for acceptance. "Sometimes parents need to be alone," he said.

Robbie didn't answer.

"Don't they ever take you anywhere?"

"Sometimes. Overnight places. Not on their long trips, like to Hawaii."

Will turned around and fitted the oars in the locks again. "Well, you've had your boat ride," he said.

"Do we have to go back so soon?"

"I have class to teach, and you have somewhere you are supposed to be." He maneuvered the boat around and headed back toward camp, rowing faster. He noted that the clouds were thickening, turning gray, covering more of the sky, and remembered a forecast of rain and possible thunder showers. He didn't like rainy camp days. They were much too gloomy.

He tied the boat at the dock and extended his hand to Robbie to help him out and saw Perry coming down the path.

Will retrieved his oars and fishing rods, took Robbie's life jacket and said, "Get going, Rob. We must be a little late."

He met Perry at the end of the dock.

"Miss Lucey was around looking for you, Mr. Bonneville. She's a little annoyed with you."

Will smiled at him. *Good.*

"Well, she wondered where you were so I had to tell her."

Will patted his arm. "Can't tell fibs, Perry. I'll go up and see what she wants."

"I didn't tell her Rob was with you. Someone else did that."

Will wondered which of Rob's cabin-mates had done so, since there wasn't anyone else, but didn't ask. "Come on, Mick. We'll go together."

The dog walked beside him, wagging his tail, while he returned the oars and life jackets to their racks, put the fishing rods in his office in Kaflik, and started up the hill toward Miss Lucey's office, which was located at one end off the dining hall.

Will regarded what had once been a nineteenth century farmhouse with distaste. It was still white, still clapboarded, but it looked too much like what it was, offices and store rooms, to retain much more than a fleeting memory of its past. He had long thought that they could have done a better job with the remodeling, used better taste. The dining hall and infirmary were in an addition that did not match the older parts. At the bottom of the steps he told Mick to stay put, walked up the three steps to the wide porch, and opened the door thinking, this must be just a little like what Robbie must have felt when he was brought here. Will squashed the feeling. There was nothing Miss Lucey could do to him now, whatever she might say. He pulled open her office door after knocking once.

Amanda Lucey was sitting at her desk busy with the pile of papers in front of her, and obviously annoyed at the interruption of his entry.

Will asked, as pleasantly as he could manage, "You wanted to see me, Miss Lucey?"

She pulled herself up straight and glared at him. "Yes, I wanted to see you. Don't you know what the camp rules are?"

"Probably as well as you do."

"Then you know that non-swimmers don't go out in the boats."

Will smiled at her. "Rob's learning. Besides, he was perfectly safe."

"Rules are rules, Mr. Bonneville."

"Rules occasionally need to be bent a little. Robbie is a little different from your regular campers, and he had a need for that trip."

"Then he should learn to swim like everyone else."

"He will eventually maybe. He's non-buoyant and can't float."

"Everyone can learn to swim."

"It took me a long time, too."

"That is beside the point. Besides"— she leveled her finger at him—"that boy is on probation because of the smoking incident yesterday. You should know that. You brought him in here."

"Rob wasn't smoking. The others dragged him up there."

"Then why did you bring him in with the others?"

"It was necessary, for his own good."

"I think you take a bit too much on yourself, Mr. Bonneville."

"Maybe." He was finding it hard to keep his tone light and his smile in place. "I rarely get involved with your campers, but this one interests me."

"Then get uninterested, Mr. Bonneville. Rules have to be followed, or we can have a lot of trouble. You've given him the idea that he doesn't have to do as he's told. There's no telling what he might do next, and I can't send him home because his parents are in Bermuda."

Will thought of Robbie's unloved grandfather and smiled again. "Rob won't break any rules, Miss Lucey, but I can't vouch for the others in his cabin."

"Are you guaranteeing that?" The skepticism in her voice bordered on sarcasm.

Will ignored her tone and insinuations. "That Rob will stay out of trouble? No, just that he won't be the cause of it. Left alone, he'd never let you know he was here. His cabinmates are a different type. They want Rob in trouble."

She laughed at him. "You are giving boys too much credit. Boys that age don't think that far."

"That far and further."

"I think you are exaggerating, Mr. Bonneville, because you happen to like Robbie."

He was fast losing his control of his voice. "Maybe, but Rob is different from them, different in the way he thinks and acts, and they have been taught to despise anyone who is different."

"Oh, come now. They're just boys."

He heard the derision in her voice and it grated. "Children are the cruelest people in the world. Anyone who thinks or looks different is a threat to their world, and to their parents' world. You have to conform, to be the same. Rob doesn't and thinks he can't be."

"He doesn't look any different from the rest. He comes from a perfectly normal home. We make sure of that before we accept them here."

"So you won't have any trouble," Will said. "No, he just feels differently, looks at things a little differently. Mainly, he doesn't like sports."

Miss Lucey shuffled the pile of papers on her desk again, apparently wanting Will gone, to finish this distressing conversation.

"Perry said you were looking for me when you discovered I was out fishing. Did you want something?"

She looked up again, in control again, her eyes frosty. "Yes. I wished to discuss your relationship with Miss Conley. I don't think it is seemly."

Will laughed, a cold, brittle laugh, and thought fleetingly of Perry and Joyce as he had seen them in Perry's cabin. Was that seemly? "Not seemly? We are adults and whatever relationship we happen to have is our business."

She met his eyes and did not give ground. "Not here, it isn't. We have to consider our young charges."

Will smiled again, genuinely this time and finding wry humor in the situation. "Seeing that at the end of this camp season I will no longer be in your employ, I don't feel obliged to submit to your tyrannies any longer. Miss Conley and I are engaged to be married. We will both be leaving."

She could not entirely hide her disbelief.

Will said pleasantly as he opened the door, "And I will be returning to my former position with the state forestry service. You will have to find another watchman. Good day, Miss Lucey."

He went back out into the sunshine, called to his dog, and went up the hill to his cabin, feeling much better about life than he had in months. He had only one class this afternoon and that was inside with a group of the youngest girls. With no more walking today, nothing to cause more problems, he would make it through all right.

But there were some things he needed to find out, for his peace of mind and Shannon's, and he knew where the answers were.

When Will and Mick walked down the long hill later that evening, there were a few night lights in the dining room and the infirmary wing, but the camp offices were dark. Will knew where he was going and did not use his flashlight. Amanda Lucey had gone back to her small house on the edge of the camp some time ago and was unlikely to return to her office until morning. As the camp caretaker, he had keys to everything and entering her office was no problem. When he was inside, away from the windows facing the camp, he switched on his pocket light and located the file cabinet. A moment's search of campers' records produced what he was looking for: Robbie's registration card.

He sat down in Miss Lucey's desk chair to read it, using only his pocket light. Camp Rocky Point pretended to an exclusivity it did not have and registration forms were detailed, asking for information of little use to the camp directors. Will read Robbie's card, filled out in a known but almost forgotten hurried scrawl, with growing disbelief, and heart ache.

Father: Morey Carter Sullivan. Mother: Carol Ambrose Sullivan. Birth date . . .

He stopped, his chest tightening, remembering dates, calculating times. Carol had probably been three months pregnant when he had last seen her.

He knew Carol had been seeing Morey Sullivan for some time, he didn't know how long of course, but wasn't she too smart for that? She had always said . . .

He put the card away, closed the file, and went back out again, locking the door behind him. He headed blindly for Shannon's cabin, the familiar tightness beginning to squeeze his chest, the tearing pain of angina. He breathed deeply, trying to relax and relieve the pain, but the realization was overwhelming. Robbie just might be his son. It would explain so much if he were: the similarity of interests, the color of their hair, perhaps even Will's attraction to the boy. But that was a romantic notion. He told himself, tried to convince himself, things like this just don't happen in real life, this is just an unhappy coincidence.

He collapsed on Shannon's step and leaned against the railing trying to catch his breath. Mick barked sharply once, and Shannon opened the door. She was beside him immediately, her arms around him, holding him tight against her. "Will? Will, what happened?"

The seizure eased as he relaxed, as it usually did, and he decided he didn't need a pill. "I got nosey," he said. "Never get nosey, Shan. It doesn't pay."

"Will, what are you talking about?"

He told her. "I guess I had to know."

Her arms tightened around him, but she didn't speak.

"It was a bit of a shock," he said. "Carol never wanted any children at all. So who is Rob, his son or mine?"

She pressed her face against his shoulder but said nothing.

"It makes no difference, does it?" he asked, knowing that it could make a great deal of difference to him.

She shook her head. "Not to me, Will. I love you, regardless, and I can love Robbie as well. You do already." She added after a moment, "All of that is in the past."

"But what difference would it make to Rob, if he knew?"

"How would he know unless his mother told him? If he thinks he's a Sullivan, his mother must think that is what he is."

"I meant, to know that his mother was once married to me."

"Maybe he knows."

"No, he doesn't know. I'm sure of that."

"Do you plan to tell him?"

"No, that isn't my place."

"And it won't make any difference in how you feel about him?"

That one he couldn't answer. "I don't know."

She asked, in her brisk professional nurse tone, "Has the pain eased?"

"Yes, I can get up now."

She straightened but kept her arm around him. "Will, I get so scared sometimes."

He tried to smile at her. "I told you," he said, not much more than a whisper, "I don't have a terribly long life left."

She slipped both arms around his neck and kissed him. "But I will share that time with you. However long it is."

"Or short." He held her close again, his face against the side of her neck. He was not being fair to her, but he could not let her go. Tomorrow he would think about Carol and Robbie who had turned out to be her son, but not now.

Will was awakened in the deep of the night by the sound of thunder. He listened to it, decided the storm was following the hills around the farther side of the pond, and there was no need for him to get up. In cases of severe storms, campers were gathered in unit houses and the dining hall, fires were lit in the fireplaces, sometimes corn was popped, hot chocolate prepared. Emergencies were handled that way, quietly, efficiently, not alarming the children.

It occurred to him as he fell asleep again. *That's what will be done if something happens to me.* He told himself firmly, *But it's not going to, not now when I again have a future, and it isn't here.*

17. ROBBIE

Robbie took his newfound courage in hand and said quite firmly and steadily, "I don't want to play ball."

Mr. Perry frowned and regarded him silently for a moment. "Really? And what do you intend to do instead?"

Robbie was holding a small paperback book in his hand, a field guide to the identification of trees of the northeastern United States that he had borrowed from Kaflik. He held it toward his unit leader. "Mr. Bonneville said I should study this."

Mr. Perry grunted and turned away. "Well, all right then but stay in sight so I'll know where you are. Don't go running off someplace."

Amazed and gratified by this small victory, Robbie retreated to the shade of a clump of white birches at the edge of the playing field and opened the book. Having said that he was going to study it, he started reading and soon became engrossed in it, in the subtle differences between the dozen or more types of wild cherries. He hadn't known there were so many kinds. He didn't pay any more attention to the ball players until they trooped past him noisily on the way back to their cabins and Mr. Perry spoke to him.

"Come along, Robbie, you need exercise, too."

A while later he was at the end of a straggling line of hikers on another nature walk. He was too far behind to really hear what Mr. Bonneville was saying, but he made no effort to move closer. Today he didn't want to call any attention to himself. He kept the memory of the wonderful and so unexpected boat ride in a safe place in his heart where he could bring it out and examine when he was alone, reliving the gentle rocking motion of the rowboat; the invigorating sensation of the cool water pushing on his fingers as they moved through the little waves; watching the little fish darting in and out among the water plants on the pond bottom; remembering Sir Richard's soft fur against his face.

He could find no reason for the excursion, for Mr. Bonneville to break a rule for him, especially after the previous day's disaster behind the old barn. It was not because his leader was pleased with him. Mr. Bonneville had been very angry.

His cabin-mates had made much of that short trip, laughing at him, calling him Mr. Bonneville's pet, and asking why he was so privileged, although he knew that they were all swimmers and any of them could go out on the lake whenever rowing was offered, as it was occasionally during free time. Both rowing and canoe classes were available to certified swimmers. None of them, apparently, had interest enough to take part.

Robbie, not inclined to hurry today, strolled along the gently rising path they were climbing to where their leader had stopped and was pointing out something on a large tree, and wished he were a little closer so that he could hear. Mr. Bonneville glanced in his direction, but turned away and moved on without more than a hint of recognition. It was enough for Robbie, however, to take as encouragement. He walked a little faster up the path, past several of the other boys, and found himself a new place much closer to the head of the line, when the group moved on again.

The afternoon was warm and sunny with only a few high thin clouds. They were in the open, following a rutted path through what had once been a high pasture full of field daisies, yellow and orange hawkweeds, and the first of the black-eyed susans and Queen Anne's lace. Robbie absorbed his surroundings as he usually did, the pleasant warmth on his back, the enticing aroma of the sunbaked ground and the drying grass, and found himself wishing for a big red dog to walk with. He looked around self-consciously afraid he had spoken that wish aloud, but no one was paying any attention to him. He returned his full attention to what the counselor was saying.

"Erosion," he heard Mr. Bonneville say, "would be a major problem on this hillside if it weren't for the thick sod. That is one reason why it was used as a pasture, or hay field, rather than a garden."

Robbie looked back along the hill they had just climbed, noted the weathered gray granite ledges that protruded through the grass and wondered if water had washed them free of soil that had once covered them, or if they had always stuck out that way as the soil built up around them. He turned to ask, but their leader was too far away.

"Take five," Mr. Bonneville said.

Robbie noted that with both surprise and concern that his face seemed pale, tight as if he might be in pain. He watched Mr. Bonneville settle himself carefully on an outcropping of granite, rest his elbows on his knees, and stare out over the valley below them. Robbie wanted very much to go to him, to sit beside him, to ask his questions about the erosion, but he turned away and found another place to sit, a place of soft grass beside a ledge, where he could see his leader, and was not close to anyone.

There were butterflies flitting in the weeds below him, little ones of sky blue and others pale yellow. He recognized the sulphurs and a common blue and it gave him a warm satisfied feeling that he could now identify them. Beyond them he saw another, larger butterfly, yellow and black striped, a tiger swallowtail flitting from hawkweed to tall buttercup, wild flowers that he could also now name. Beside him on a blade of grass, a large beetle was making its slow way toward the tuft on top. He watched it, fascinated by the iridescent blue-black shine of its ungainly body.

A midsized butterfly fluttered past him, one he had never seen before, mottled yellow, orange and brown, with spots on its upper forewings sort of like a red admiral. He recalled Mr. Bonneville's comment that you could call them flutterbys, a word play that had amused him enough to remember.

He watched the butterfly, trying to remember its markings so that he could find it in the guide book he had, once again, forgotten to bring with him.

"That one is a painted lady," Mr. Bonneville said from behind him. "They usually come out a little later in the summer."

Robbie glanced sideways at him. "I never heard of that kind."

"Then you didn't read the book very well. They are very common."

His brusque tone hurt a little and Robbie went back to watching the big shiny beetle.

"But I don't suppose you can remember them all in a few days' study. It does take a few seasons to see them all and there are a lot of variations." Mr. Bonneville rested his hand on the ledge beside him. "Tell me, Rob, what did you do with that picture you took of me? Miss Conley said it was pretty good."

Robbie hesitated, wondering at the question. "I sent it to my mother. I wasn't planning to, but I did, kind of scooped them all up and put them in the letter." He turned to face his leader. "I can take another one if you want me to."

He thought the counselor looked ill. "Mr. Bonneville, it's all right, isn't it? You don't mind that I took it?"

"No, it's okay, Rob. I just wondered." He pushed himself upright and turned away. "All right, you guys, let's get going."

They formed a line again, laughing, jostling each other, and continued up the hill. Mr. Bonneville stopped suddenly. "Mr. Dan, why don't you take the boys up to the top of the hill and enjoy the view?"

"Up there?" Mr. Dan pointed to a point some distance above them where there was no real path among the out-jutting ledges and small juniper bushes, and to where Mr. Bonneville had never taken them.

"Why not? It's a good climb and will use up some of their excess energy. I'll meet you on your way back down. It's a good day for it and nobody is interested in lichens and mosses today anyway."

Mr. Dan laughed. "Come on, you guys, I'll beat you to the top."

They left with war whoops, racing each other, scrambling up the rocky hillside.

Mr. Bonneville said, "You, too, Rob."

Robbie eyed the steepness of the slope and shook his head. "Do I have to?"

"It would do you good."

"I'd rather stay here and talk to you."

Mr. Bonneville was still watching the group now almost half way to the top.

Robbie again found his new courage. "You told me to stand up for what I wanted to do."

Mr. Bonneville chuckled. "So I did. Shall we walk up the path to meet them or wait here?"

Robbie hesitated, glancing around the old pasture and down the hill before making up his mind. He thought his counselor looked tired, sick maybe. "Let's sit under a tree."

"You probably sit under way too many trees and don't do half enough hill climbing."

Robbie kept his gaze on the hill climbers now almost out of sight. "Now you sound like my father."

Mr. Bonneville made an odd sound, almost a choke, and Robbie looked up in alarm, but he didn't dare ask if anything were wrong.

Mr. Bonneville laughed again, a harsh strangling sound that frightened Robbie a little. "All right," he said, his voice normal again, kind and gentle as Robbie liked it. "Let's just stand under that choke cherry tree. The others won't be long getting to the top and back."

Robbie decided he had imagined the last few minutes and everything was fine. He led the way into the shade of the cherry tree, leaned against the trunk and tried to remember why this cherry was different from several others, but he didn't ask.

"Just enjoy the day," Mr. Bonneville said. "Before it rains again."

Robbie wondered at the comment, if maybe it meant something else, but he asked instead about the erosion. That seemed a much safer topic.

18. WILFRED

"Robbie sent the picture he took of me to his mother," Will told Shannon as they sat on his cabin steps later that evening. He hoped his frustration wasn't showing too much and that he could stay relaxed enough to prevent a seizure. He could sometimes keep the pain at bay through determination, while he accomplished something he needed to do, but he frequently couldn't. He was afraid that this was one of those times, events he could not control.

"Now what do I do?" he asked. "What will she think or do? I haven't seen nor heard from her since the divorce. I haven't wanted to."

He knew that wasn't quite true. In the beginning, when she was newly gone, he had wanted very much to see her, to know why she had left him, betrayed his trust, rejected his offered love, what it was that he had done or failed to do. Then he'd still loved her and his pain was new, deep and raw. Now he had Shannon and it didn't matter. Or it hadn't mattered until Robbie.

"What can you do, Will, besides be somewhere else when they come to pick up Robbie? When she sees the picture, she will know, anyway, and Robbie will talk about you. Isn't anything more up to her? If she wants to see you, won't she come looking for you when she gets here?"

He laughed even though he could see no humor in the situation. He foresaw only more hurt for all of them and he wanted to avoid it, especially for Robbie who could be hurt very much, and Shannon who was hurting already. "I doubt they will come and look me up. Why would they? After all these years?"

He added to himself, except maybe she's curious. I wonder what she looks like now? Does she ever think about me?

"I suppose it will depend a lot on what Robbie told her in the letter he wrote to her," Shannon said thoughtfully. "He probably raved about how wonderful you are and about all those nature things you've been teaching him."

He heard the sadness in her voice that she was trying to hide and it hurt. He didn't want her hurting, too. "All the more reason to let me hide." He paused, sighed. "As I've been hiding from it all of these years."

"Unless, of course—"

"Yes. Unless." He didn't want to think about that possibility, about all that he had missed, the lost years if Robbie were his, or about all he would be losing in the future, knowing Robbie was out of reach. He told himself firmly he didn't really want to know the truth. Not now. It was too late for him and Robbie, no matter what the truth was. *It will be better for Robbie if I just disappear from his life again. I've never been a part of it and now I can't be. But how will it be for me? Now that I've met him? And how will Shannon feel about all this? What difference will it make to her? And if we have children, what about them, shouldn't they know? Robbie didn't know his other half-siblings and it didn't seem to bother him.*

"I had a talk with Rob this afternoon during our hike," he said, suppressing his inner doubts and finding a more cheerful topic. "I think all he needs is someone to talk to once in awhile."

"What did you talk about?"

"Nothing, really. Look, Shan"—he turned and faced her, his concerns surfacing again—"suppose he does find out that his mother and I used to be married. He doesn't get along with his own father all the time, so suppose he decided to think . . ." He didn't go on with the thought. It was too painful, and he could see Shannon was following his reasoning. "And that can't be, can't ever happen, no matter what. It would be better for all of us if he just forgets about me. I'm leaving this camp, so there won't be any chance of his seeing me again."

But, he thought, *maybe, just maybe I've given him a little help, a way to cope better with his life. I can remember that and he can remember me, or my advice.*

She nodded, but he could see the misery in her eyes, the tears she was trying not to shed. "Will, this is all so unfair to you. Robbie knows you now, likes you, admires you. How can he forget that? Won't his mother see that?"

He had thought about that, too, and tried to dismiss it. "Carol was never too concerned about anybody but herself."

"But if Robbie is your son, why didn't she ever tell him?"

He recalled the last time he had seen her, mostly naked and in bed, his bed, with another man, and closed his mind to that scene. "Who knows? I don't think I'll ever ask her. I don't think I could." He added what he had been telling himself ever since he had read the registration card. "She never mentioned me because Robbie is Morey's. Why should she do any different? Even if she was married to me at the time?"

"But he is too like you in too many ways for it to be a coincidence. Of course, I've never seen Sullivan."

He knew Morey Sullivan to be a large, dark-haired athletic-looking man, and Robbie was slim and blond, more like Carol. "Coincidence it has to be, Shan. And Robbie has to think that I was just a counselor who took an interest in him for a couple of weeks. There is no other choice." He put his arm around her and held her against him. "There is only you and me."

She nodded silently.

"Just as soon as this camp session is ended we can both start over. Somewhere else." He wondered fleetingly if that were really true. Could he really go back to that other life? At least they wouldn't be living here but farther north.

"But it is so unfair. To both of you. To everyone."

The sadness and bitterness in her voice cut deep in his heart and he wondered if she should have added, and so unfair to me? "That's life, I guess," he said. "I can't see any other course. I have to think about him, don't I? What's best for him? No matter how much I like him, what I might hope for, it can't be. It's way too late. I know that, you know that."

"I know that, Will, but it doesn't make it right for either of you."

He held her in his arms against his chest and silently cursed Carol and the fate that had brought her son to Camp Rocky Point.

Somehow he would get through the last week and it would be the last week for Robbie. He would just have to make their contacts, their conversations, shorter and fewer, to make it easier. For both of them.

19. ROBBIE

With supper over and quieter evening activities being planned before bedtime, dusk was gathering in deep shadowy pools under the row of trees between the lines of cabins. The bright evening star twinkled in the deep blue of the western sky above the tree line across the lake. A gentle breeze had risen and stirred the air, cooling it from the heat and humidity of the day, but it was still softly warm, inviting one outside. Robbie sat on the cabin steps enjoying being alone after a full day of crafts, archery and first aid, all a lot fun and interesting, but he wanted to be alone for awhile to consider all that had happened. His cabin-mates had gone, as usual, to play ball of some sort, although it was getting too dark for baseball.

Robbie had stayed behind to think about the past few days, to sort out a great many conflicting impressions and emotions. His quiet exchange with Mr. Bonneville while the others climbed the hill, for instance, and how nice it had been to have questions answered, without being asked why he was asking them. Sitting still and watching the fading light in the sky, he remembered how comfortable it had made him. , He relished how different it had been to talk to someone like himself for a change, somebody who seemed to understand.

And then there was the wonderful boat ride a few days ago, the realization of a long held fervent wish, granted so unexpectedly, and when he was in trouble, no less, on probation for the smoking fiasco he did not want to think about. He leaned forward, put his elbows on his knees, and rested his chin in his hands as he recalled the sensation of the cold lake water against his hand as they moved through the water and the dog's head resting companionably against his knee. Mr. Bonneville's sure easy strokes had propelled them so smoothly through the water, apparently so effortlessly. He wished he could row a boat like that, wished he had a boat, or one he could use sometimes. It was what he had wanted to do for years, since he had first seen row boats and canoes on television, but his parents had no interest. And he was going to leave it all at the end of next week. He covered his face with his hands and allowed his sadness to engulf him but he refused to cry, he would not give in to tears even when life was so cruelly unfair. He had been teased too often about his tears.

He was jerked back to the present reality as his cabinmates were suddenly all around him, laughing and pointing at him. He saw their mocking, grinning faces and panic hit his stomach like a hard fist making it hard to breathe. There was an obvious tension around them, a suppressed excitement. He knew they were planning something for him, to do to him, and it wasn't going to be anything good. He scrambled awkwardly to his feet, tripping over the bottom step as he did so, trying to retreat into the cabin where he might be able to close and bar the door. He knew it was a faint hope but there was no place else for him to go, no place to hide, no one to call to for help, but he had to try.

Corey laughed at him, a cold harsh, totally unfriendly sound, and caught his arm, pulling him to his feet. "You're coming with us, Robbie."

"Where?"

"You'll see. Come on, guys."

They surrounded him still laughing, tugging and propelling him along the path, keeping him in their midst. They were headed in the general direction of the wash house giving Robbie visions of being held in a cold shower, but he could stand that. It had happened before.

But his captors veered off the path as soon as they were behind the row of cabins, out of the sight of their counselor who was presumably with the game players, and up the hill toward the old barn. He dug in his heels, fought against them, resisting as best he could. Cold fear gripped him. He didn't want to go there again. But Sam had one arm and Art the other, holding tight and pulling him along with them. Bert and Joe were behind him, pushing him, keeping him close behind Corey who led the way through the deepening dusk.

Corey's voice reached him, menacingly quiet and insistent, "And keep your mouth shut, Robbie. One peep out of you and you'll get it from all of us. We're going in the barn, and you're coming in with us. Understand? We don't have very long before Mr. Perry'll be coming back and looking for us, and we have to be back at the cabin by then."

Robbie fully understood but he still looked around for a means of escape. He saw none. He asked, "Why? Why do I have to go with you? I won't tell on you."

"We like your company, Robbie. You never do anything with us. We're all mates, aren't we? Supposed to do stuff together?"

"Well, I don't like yours." He tried to put all of his dislike into his tone.

Art snickered. "We know. You'd rather be with Mr. Bonneville or somebody, studyin' ferns or birds or something. Not this time, buddy, you come with us. You're a boy, not a girl."

That jibe hurt. He had heard it too often. "Can't you get into enough trouble by yourselves? You don't need me."

"Who's to know? You might tell somebody."

"I said I wouldn't. Let me go back to our cabin. I'll keep Mr. Perry from looking for you. Honest."

"Too late for that," Corey said. "We're already here. Art, get the door open and inside before someone sees us."

The flat wooden door was pulled open and Art and Bert scrambled through, stepping over the mid-calf-high door sill into the darkness inside. Staring through that gaping opening into a seeming black void, Robbie was overwhelmed by a mind-numbing dread. He knew, with a deep surety, something awful was about to happen to him, to all of them, and he couldn't stop it. The boy behind him shoved him into the blackness of the interior, and he was hit by the musty odor of dust and dry wood. The others stumbled through the doorway and pulled the door shut behind them. Faint daylight showed through the upper windows but did not reach into the blackness where Robbie stood nearly paralyzed with fright.

Where's that candle?" Corey said calmly from beside him. He struck a match from a paper match book. It flared with exaggerated brightness for a moment, then steadied as he applied it to the wick of a small candle Bert was holding, apparently pulled from a pocket. Robbie recognized it from a craft project earlier in the week and realized that Bert had stolen it. Candles were among the forbidden items in cabins. *How long have they been planning this?*

In spite of himself, now that his eyes had adjusted a little to the dimness, Robbie looked around with curiosity and he lost some of the paralysis that had gripped his limbs. The space around him was full of shadowy things he could not identify in the flickering light. The candle illuminated only a tiny circle of light around Bert as he stepped carefully across the floor. Corey's hand urged Robbie forward toward that light and he saw ahead of him a flight of open steps along one wall, not much more than a slanted ladder, leading to a platform higher up where he knew hay had once been stored. He glanced behind him and saw the outline of the door through which they had come, the dimming light outside showing through the cracks. It seemed to him it was a possible means of escape if he could get back to it without the others noticing him in the dark.

He took one short pace away from Corey toward the door, stopped, waited a moment, holding his breath. The others were busy inspecting piles of things on the other side of the stairs. He moved another quick and silent step and waited again, listening to the other boys, and then another furtive step, another wait. The door was a few feet away, only another step or two. He moved quickly and he almost made it.

"Where's Robbie?" Corey asked suddenly.

Robbie scrambled toward the door, hoping the darkness would hide him, but he stumbled on something he didn't see and nearly fell. He lurched forward, one hand touching the door, but Art's hands closed around his arm as he reached it. Art and Bert dragged Robbie back to Corey in spite of his protestations and best efforts.

"Let me go. This is all wrong. You know it is."

"That was dumb, Robbie. Why don't you do like we told you? Now I have to do something with you. We can't let you go now." Corey turned, looking around him. "Bring him over here." He walked toward the flight of steps.

They dragged Robbie there, twisted his arms behind him, around the post at the bottom of the stairs, and Sam tied his hands with a piece of string Bert had in his pocket. He pulled the string tight enough to hurt, and Robbie yelped.

"That hurts. What are you doing? Let me go?"

Corey laughed at him. "That should hold you for a few minutes. I warned you, Robbie. Come on, guys, let's look this place over. We don't have much time. Mr. Perry'll come looking for us or blow his whistle or something, and we don't want to get caught up here."

Robbie watched the flickering circle of candle light move up the stairs, then slowly around the old hay loft, the tiny flame the only light in the smothering darkness. His wrists hurt, his hands were growing numb, and his arms were cramped. He tried again, desperately, to free himself, but the knots were too tight for him to move. Although he could feel that whatever held him was not very heavy, simply a piece of cotton string, he couldn't break it. Trying cut into his wrists.

The boys came slowly back down the steps, inching their way in the uncertain light. "Nothing up there," Bert said in disgust. "All of this planning for nothing. I thought there'd be some good stuff in here. What do they keep all this junk locked up for?"

Art asked, laughing, "How you doing, Robbie? You should have gone up there with us. It's like a ghost walk on Halloween."

Robbie refused to answer, and Bert laughed.

"Well, there's not much here after all," Corey said. "This was a waste of time. Come on. Let's get out of here before somebody misses us."

"We going to take him along, too?" Bert asked.

"We can't leave him here. Somebody'd find him and then he'd have to tell how he got here and all tied up."

Robbie looked beyond him to where Sam and Joe were noisily investigating the far back corner of the room with the now very small candle providing little light.

Corey turned that way, following his gaze.

"Give me the candle, Sam," Joe said. "There's something over here in this box that looks funny."

Sam reached across the boxes, but Joe's fingers slipped on the candle stub. The candle fell into the box at Sam's feet. Joe yelled, reached for it, but it blazed up suddenly, sending a burst of flame into the air. Joe scrambled back, around the stacked boxes, and Sam was close behind him.

"Look out," Bert yelled. "Get out of here. Everything's on fire."

In their mad scramble for the door, Corey stopped beside Robbie and tugged at the strings around his wrists. The fire had died down a little but was smoldering, belching thick, dark choking smoke. "I can't see, Robbie," Corey said, his voice full of fear. "Sam tied it too tight." He tugged at the cord hurting Robbie's hands and not loosening the binding. "I can't see the knots."

The fire suddenly flared up again, igniting another pile of the wooden boxes. The flames crackled and rose higher at an alarming rate of speed.

Corey tugged at the knots again, accomplishing nothing. Robbie could not find his voice. He stared at the fire creeping toward them and choked on the smoke.

Corey backed away from him. "I can't get it undone, Robbie. Oh, God, I'm sorry, Robbie. I'm so sorry." He turned and stumbled away from him toward the door now standing open.

Robbie stared after him. "Corey, come back. Help me!" He looked at the fire again. "Corey! Somebody! Help me!

Corey stopped once more just inside the door. "I can't, Robbie. I'll find somebody. I promise."

He was gone, and Robbie started to cry, choking on the smoke and his sobs, still calling for Corey, for somebody to come, but he got no answer. There was no longer any fresh air, just the roiling smoke, and it was getting very hard to breathe.

20. WILFRED

It was almost full dark when Will left Kaflik and started up the hill toward his cabin. It had been a long day, exhausting physically with an unusual three walks scheduled. He usually avoided making more than two excursions, but one was a rescheduled girls' ramble to look at wildflowers that had been postponed by wet grass. It was a very easy and quite enjoyable stroll through meadows, but twice he had come close to considering medication. The spasms had passed quickly, apparently with no one noticing his discomfort.

I really do have to get out of this place. It's killing me. What I need now is a good cup of coffee and to sit with Shannon for a while and unwind, no more exertions.

Emotionally he was drained, wrung dry, hollowed out, and he was trying not to think about the past few days, or what the future might hold. He had avoided Robbie all day, not wanting to see him, not wanting even to think about him. He felt ill. *If I can get back to my cabin, get rested, sit with Shannon, and talk about this I'll be okay.*

He walked slowly, ignoring his surroundings, but suddenly there were sounds to his left farther up the hill, people running, boys' voices yelling with an undercurrent of terror. He could not see who it was, but he turned that way thinking, *Kids up by the barn, damn 'em. Why can't someone else handle this?*

And again the thought, *Why didn't I take care of that before camp started like I should have?*

He smelled the acrid smoke before he reached the barn, before Corey came out of the gloom, crying, and clutched desperately at him. "Robbie," he gasped, choking. "Robbie's in the barn."

The barn door was open, a red glow showing evilly behind the roiling smoke pouring out. "Where?" Panic hit his constricting chest and the pit of his stomach. "The barn's on fire! Where is he?"

"Tied to the post at the bottom of the stairs." There was stark fear in the boy's voice. "We didn't mean to. Honest, Mr. Bonneville."

Will didn't want to listen to explanations. "Tied?" He could hear the crackling of the fire now, and thick smoke rolled out of the open door.

"We tied him up so he wouldn't run away and tell on us."

"Go get Miss Conley to sound the alarm. Send her up here. I'll get Robbie."

He was already running up the hill, fumbling for the jacknife he always kept in his pocket. He hesitated a moment in the barn door. The smoke was too thick to see through, but he stepped over the high threshold orienting himself as he did so. The stairs were on the left. "Rob? Robbie, where are you?"

Will heard the sounds of coughing and choking and turned that way. Although the flames made it light enough to see, it was too hot and there was too much thick smoke. Will shuffled toward the sounds. Robbie was there, tied to the post as Corey had said. Finding the cords around his wrists and cutting him free took only a moment. Then Will had the boy by the arm, pulling him, stumbling away from the heat of the spreading fire toward the open door, to be out of the thick smoke into fresh air and the safety that was only a few steps away.

"Come on, Robbie. It'll be okay."

The pain in his chest was sudden and sharp, cutting through his chest like a knife, pain like he had never felt before. Will stopped, unable to move while he tried to breathe, to draw a breath not filled with the thick strangling smoke. He cried out, stumbled, fell to one knee, and could not get up.

He wheezed between choking breaths, "Go on, Rob, get out of here."

But Robbie didn't go. He put both hands around Will's arm and pulled. "Get up, Mr. Bonneville. Come on, it's only a few steps."

"I can't, Rob. Go on."

"Not without you." Robbie was coughing, choking on the smoke, but he continued to tug on his arm. The fire was getting closer and had reached the loft over their heads, crackling angrily and raining sparks into the ground floor. "Get up. I'll help you. You can do it."

The pain was intense and getting worse, but his fear for Robbie gave him a measure of strength and a will to move. He forced himself up, took two uncertain steps, and stumbled again, the pain tearing at his chest. "Go on, Rob, run, get out."

The fire was close behind them, spreading along the dry wooden floor, the deadly smoke thick and overpowering. Robbie pulled insistently on his arm, trying to get him onto his feet again. "Please get up, Mr. Bonneville. I can't leave you." He was coughing, choking.

Will forced himself up again, for Robbie's sake, though the pain was engulfing him, making it hard to think. *I have to get Robbie out.*

"Only a little further," Robbie pleaded, his desperation growing plainer. "Come on."

Will took another hesitant step and tried to ignore an unbearable surge of pain. Robbie's pleading, tearful voice kept urging him on, and he took one more step. The heat of the fire was close behind, the suffocating smoke was all around them, and then there was a cooling breath of fresh air.

Shannon's voice reached him, calling, pleading. Hands grabbed his arms and helped him over the doorsill, and he knew Robbie was safe.

And then there was nothing.

21. SHANNON

Shannon stood in the hospital visitors' waiting room with Will's brother Edward, a Styrofoam cup of now cold and barely tasted coffee in her hand. The window beside her overlooked the crowded parking lot but she wasn't really seeing what was there. She was much too tired and too uncertain of the future.

"It's been over twenty-four hours," she said, the strain of those hours in her voice. "Every hour he lives makes his chances that much better."

"What are his chances now?"

She shook her head, not looking at him. Edward had arrived only a few minutes ago and she didn't know how to talk to him, what to tell him.

"Are they going to operate?"

She turned around and faced him. He looked a lot more like Will than he had led her to believe. Ed had a much heavier build but the same blond hair and sensitive face. His fear and concern were obvious. "If he stabilizes, and I think they said he has. The doctor said there is a very good chance they can correct most of the damage to his heart." She hesitated, wondering if she should ask, but she wanted to know and so did the surgeon. "Why didn't he have surgery before? When he had the first attack?"

"He refused it, said he didn't think a fifty-percent chance was good enough odds to go through an expensive operation."

"I'm not surprised. That is something he would do."

Edward didn't dispute that. "And I don't think he cared, back then."

She put her unwanted coffee cup on a small table. "I hope, think, he does now."

"So do I." After a long pause, he asked, "Can I see him?"

"When he wakes up again, I think we can go in. He's been in and out of consciousness for the past few hours. The last time I talked to him I told him you were coming." She covered her eyes with her hand. "I don't know if he understood, but I think he did."

"Why don't you sit down? You look all in."

She shook her head. "I've been sitting with him, kind of napping." *If I sit I'll fall asleep, and I can't sleep yet, not until I know he will be all right.*

Edward sat on the arm of an upholstered chair. "I went out to his cabin and picked up Mick and the cat. Mick knows me so he'll be okay. Somebody had been up there and fed them, some young guy named Dan. He was very upset. I thought he was going to come undone."

"One of the counselors. Nice young man. They did a lot together."

Edward stood up again and paced around the room. He paused by the window looking out into the parking lot . "So, tell me what happened? Something about a fire in an old barn? Some kids set it and left one of them inside somehow?"

She told him as much as she knew of it, with few details since she knew none, but explaining Robbie, who he was. "Will went into the barn to get Robbie and they got out just in time. He had the attack while he was in the barn. We had to pull him out. He could barely walk. They took Robbie somewhere to be treated for smoke inhalation and brought Will here."

She had followed the ambulance, she said, and had talked only briefly with Miss Lucey late last night. Amanda had called the hospital earlier this morning and left a message for Shannon to call the camp as soon as she had news. So far, she had none so she hadn't called. She wasn't ready yet to talk to Miss Lucey.

"I can't believe this happened," Amanda said last night. "Not here in my camp. Boys just don't do things like that. The police were quite thorough, questioning everybody, but I had to call their parents and there was a lot of confusion. The whole camp is upset, and we're sending everyone home early, just as soon as we can make arrangements."

Edward shook his head in disbelief, stopped in his pacing around the room. "All of that for Carol's son?"

Shannon didn't answer, thinking, *maybe his own son*. She rubbed at her eyes, forcing herself to stay awake a little while longer. "He would have done it for any of them."

Edward didn't argue with that. "He probably would have. He has a lot more courage than he thinks he does."

"It's a quiet kind." Edward stopped beside her. "So what happened to those boys, the ones that tied up their friend and set the barn on fire?"

"Amanda said they had been arrested, taken into custody, she called it, charged with delinquency, and released to their parents. They have to go to court whenever . . . when we know how Will makes out."

He faced her again, regarding her silently for a long moment. "You said your name is Shannon?"

"Yes. Shannon Conley. I'm the camp nurse."

"Does that happen to be my mother's antique ring you're wearing?"

She looked at it as if she had never seen it before. "Yes." She smiled at it. "Will gave it to me a few days ago."

"Have you known him long? He's never mentioned you to me, but then he never says much about himself."

"A couple of years. We are going to be married at the end of the summer." She refused to consider that it might not happen. "As soon as the camping season is over."

"I'm glad. It is about time Will had something good going for him."

"He spoke of you a couple of times. He seems to be quite fond of you."

Edward laughed. "*Fond* probably isn't the right word, but I always thought quite a bit of him. He's my big brother, you know."

"So he said. The one who defended him and fought all his battles for him."

"Not all of them. He manages pretty well on his own. I was very surprised when he took this camp job. It wasn't like him."

"He was trying to hide from everything, but he won't be going back to that camp now, even if he recovers." She paused, wondering if Will had said anything to his brother. "He was planning to go back to the Forest Service. A few days ago he got a letter from somebody telling him of a resignation and he could come back into that place. That they really wanted him back."

"I'm glad. That's where he belongs. Where he always belonged."

She said a silent prayer. *Please, God, let him recover enough.*

The door behind them opened and they both turned. The woman in the doorway was slim and coolly blond, mid-thirtyish, and her face looked much like Robbie's. She stopped in the open doorway, regarding them and not speaking.

"My God, Carol," Edward said.

She smiled thinly at him. "Hello, Ed, it's been a long time."

"It could have been a hell of a lot longer."

"Now, Ed." She looked at Shannon. "I was told you could tell me about Will, how he is." She hesitated a moment. "I thought I should come, considering he saved Robbie's life and all."

"He is holding his own," Shannon said. She was suddenly cold inside, numb, and more than a little angry. *What right does this woman have to come here? After all she's done to Will? Even if she is Robbie's mother.*

"I didn't know he had a heart attack before this one." She didn't sound particularly concerned, or interested. "And

I surely didn't know he was working at that camp. If I had, I wouldn't have sent Robbie."

"No reason why you should," Edward said coldly, his obvious anger barely suppressed. "You didn't care about him. You never did."

She regarded him steadily for a moment through lowered lashes without answering him. She took a crumpled pack of cigarettes from her purse and offered them, then took one for herself when they refused, ignoring the 'No Smoking' sign on the wall.

Shannon could see Carol's tenseness, her ill-concealed nervousness, and thawed just a little. "How's Robbie?"

"He'll be fine. They just kept him overnight to be sure about the smoke he took in. It's funny," she said, as if talking to herself, "Robbie meeting Will here. I was always going to tell him someday that Morey wasn't his real father, but I never found the right time. Seeing the picture Robbie took of him was quite a shock. To both of us."

"Why didn't you tell Will back in the beginning?" Edward asked.

She looked at him through the cigarette smoke, gazing steadily for a long minute. "Would he have believed me, considering?"

Ed laughed harshly. "Hell, no. He would have thought it was just another of your ploys to take his money. And everything else he owned."

Carol didn't answer.

Shannon asked, a little unsteadily, but needing to know for Will's sake as well as her own, "How can you be so sure Robbie is Will's, considering?"

Carol eyed Shannon a long minute, visually evaluating and wondering. "Morey had a vasectomy long before I met him. His first wife has his kids, all he ever wanted. As if he really wanted those."

Shannon had a better understanding of what Will had seen: the unwanted child. "Will has gotten rather fond of

Robbie, these last couple of weeks. They seem to have a lot in common."

Carol smiled a little, but without mirth. "Maybe Will would like to have him once in a while. It would be handy to have a place to ship him off to sometimes."

Neither Shannon nor Edward answered her.

"It would be cheaper than sending him to camp," she said. She dropped her cigarette into a potted plant on the table. "I'll tell Robbie," she continued, not looking at them, "and let him decide. If he wants to come here and see Will, I'll bring him. I don't think Will wants to see me."

Shannon didn't answer and Edward said, "Probably not."

"It will be a shock to Robbie," Carol said, then smiled at Edward. "I see you haven't changed much, and I suppose Will hasn't, either." She paused again, then turned toward the door. "Believe it or not, I really liked Will once, back then, really respected him. He was a good man." She pushed the door open then turned to look back at them. "Good-by," she said. "Tell Will for me that I'm sorry . . . about his heart attack, about everything. Sometimes I wish things had been different." She turned and was gone, closing the door behind her.

Edward swore eloquently, using a few words Shannon hadn't heard before, but she thoroughly agreed with the sentiment.

Will opened his eyes and said faintly, "My two favorite people." He closed his eyes again.

Shannon tried not to look at all of the IVs and the monitors connected to him, the tubes mostly concealed by the covering blanket, and was profoundly grateful that he was breathing on his own, even though he was still receiving oxygen. He looked so terribly thin and pale in the white bed. He had come so close to not making it. Her heart ached for him and for herself. She said as cheerfully as she could, "We're only allowed a few minutes. They don't want us to tire you out."

Edward closed his fingers over Will's hand lying limply on top of the blanket, but didn't speak.

"Don't say it, Ed," Will whispered. "I can't do anything right."

"You did it all right this time, Will. And this time the doctors are going to patch you up properly. This time you have more reasons to live than just your own stubbornness."

Will opened his eyes again, looked at Shannon and smiled crookedly.

"She's wearing Mother's opal ring. That kind of gave it away, big brother."

He closed his eyes again. "Take care of her for me, Ed, will you?"

"You'll be able to do that yourself in a little while."

Shannon hesitated, wondering what else she should say, about Carol and Robbie, how much he could stand, but he did have a right to know, and Robbie might be coming tomorrow to see him. She didn't know how to begin.

"Robbie?" Will asked. "Is he all right?"

"He's fine," Shannon said. "They checked him out for smoke inhalation, and sent him back to camp."

"His parents?"

She heard the unasked question in his voice, knew he wanted the answer but couldn't ask it

"Carol came to see how you were," Ed said. "She said to thank you for what you did for Robbie and to tell you she was sorry. For everything."

Will closed his eyes.

"She never told Robbie the truth," Shannon said. "She never told him about you, but she said she will now."

Will opened his eyes and looked at her. He said nothing, but she knew what he was thinking.

"It will be all right," Shannon said. "Believe me."

Will closed his eyes again. "Will I see him again?"

"Tomorrow," Shannon said. "If Robbie wants to come."

22. ROBBIE

Robbie took what little courage he had and went up in the hospital elevator by himself. His mother had said she would wait for him in the coffee shop and said he could stay as long as he wanted to. He knew why she didn't want to come with him, but none of it made any sense to him. He was afraid to go alone, but more afraid not to, and he had to go, had to know that Mr. Bonneville was going to be all right. He had collapsed there on the ground outside the barn and had looked almost dead when they had put into the ambulance. And nobody had told him anything until this morning. But what if he doesn't want to see me? And I have to thank him for coming into the barn and getting me free when he knew he could have a heart attack.

He thought he knew now why Mr. Bonneville had sometimes looked so tired, almost ill.

He remembered thinking how nice it would be if he found that Mr. Bonneville was a relative of some kind that he could go visit once in a while, that he could write letters to and ask his questions. But to think he was his father? Robbie wasn't sure about that part. It was almost more than he could accept: his mother had once been married to a man like Mr. Bonneville—he couldn't call him anything else yet, even to himself—and left him. He could think of no reason for it. He couldn't understand adult thinking.

"I meant to tell you one day," his mother had said, casually shrugging as if it didn't really matter. "I figured you'd never see him, so why say anything?"

"We just never got around to it," his father had added. *Only he's not really my father any more.* "You were born after your mother and I got married so it didn't make any difference."

But he had met him and liked him, Robbie thought, and now what? *What do I do now? And suppose Mr. Bonneville dies before I really get to know him?*

He didn't want to think about that, either. He didn't know very much about heart attacks, only that they were very bad, and people died of them and they usually happened to old people. Mr. Bonneville wasn't really that old, was he?

He left the elevator and stood a moment in the hallway, wondering which way to go. Then he saw Miss Conley and released a long breath. She would help him through this.

Miss Conley smiled as she came toward him. "Hello, Robbie. I was waiting for you. Your mother called and said you were on your way up."

He asked, trying to hide his growing fear, "Is Mr. Bonneville all right?"

"We're pretty sure he will be," she said. "I told him you were coming, and he's waiting for you."

"Does he know who I am? I mean . . ." He face was getting hot and knew he was turning red. "My mother told me . . ."

She smiled at him, warming and comforting him, "Yes, he knows. And we're going to have to find something for you to call him besides Mr. Bonneville."

"He doesn't mind?" Robbie asked a little fearfully. "I mean, to find out after all this time?"

"Better late than never." She stopped in front of a closed door. "You can stay with him while he's awake, but we don't want to tire him out. And he does want to see you."

She opened the door for him, held it as he walked into the dimly lighted room. He could see the bed and a lot of tubes and machines and couldn't think of anything to say. He had never been in a hospital room like this before.

"Hello, Rob," Will said softly.

Rob took two steps into the room and stopped. *Now what do I do? What do I say?*

But he remembered what Mr. Bonneville—what else can I call him?—had told him: You don't have to be afraid.

"Come here, where I can see you." His voice was weak, but kind as Robbie remembered it.

Rob took another step closer, and Shannon closed the door behind him.

"It will be all right, Rob. Believe me. We can work it out."

23. SHANNON

Shannon walked back to the elevator with Robbie. "Everything will be fine," she told him as the car door opened. We'll make arrangements for you see Will again when he is out of the hospital."

"Are you sure he'll be okay? He looks awful."

She heard the fear in his voice, all of the uncertainty, and silently agreed with him. She couldn't see their future, either, but she knew they would have one; Will would insist on it. She said, "I'm sure."

When the elevator door had closed she went back to Will. "I saw him off," she said, stopping beside his bed and closing her hand over his. "He will do all right. Did he tire you too much?"

"No." He opened his eyes and gazed up at her. "If you can accept him as well as me . . ."

She bent and kissed his cheek. "I already have, Will. I can love him as much as I love you. And I love you very much, and I was so afraid . . ."

He moved his hand enough to encircle hers. "And I love you," he whispered. "Forever."

Also from **Jessie Salisbury** and **Soul Mate Publishing**:

ORCHARD HILL

Deserted by her husband, Jocelyn fled home to the family orchard to recover and wait for her divorce to be settled. It is harvest time, and among the Nova Scotian apple pickers is Yvon, handsome, virile, devil-may-care, and more than willing to help Jocelyn forget her unfaithful spouse.

But:

There is also Adrian, her caring long-time friend and attorney. He could not speak of his love for her while she was married, but now she is free and he is ready to bring her back where she belongs. And willing to combat Yvon for her affections.

Available now on Amazon: **http://tinyurl.com/kssf9hh**